TECHNICAL HITCH

The condenser for Donzey's revolutionary FM rig blew, so he cobbled up a substitute—a piece of bone wrapped in tinfoil—then clapped the earphones on his partner.

Farrel's head tilted to one side. "Mmmwaw," he said. Then he reared out of his chair, still bleating, and started to tear the room up.

With the phones removed and the set turned off, Farrel settled down. "I saw pictures," he said wonderingly. "I was *in* those pictures. And me—and the other guys with me—we was *sheep....*"

Donzey knew he had something different in FM reception—for the bone he'd used for the condenser was a sheep bone....

BEYOND

THEODORE STURGEON

A DELL BOOK

Published by
Dell Publishing Co., Inc.
1 Dag Hammarskjold Plaza
New York, New York 10017

NEED

Some towns seem able to defy not only time, but change; when this happens in the far hinterland, one is hardly amazed. Yet, amazingly, it happens all the time quite near some of our largest cities. Occasionally one of these is found by the "project" entrepreneur, and becomes the setting for winding windrows of coops and hutches, alternately "ranch" and "split"; yet not even these, and the prefabricated, alien, chain-driven supercilious superservice shopping centers in symbiosis with them, ever become a part of such towns. Whatever span of years it takes to make the "projects" obsolescent only serves to make these towns themselves more solid, more—in the chemical sense—set. Modernity does not and cannot alter the character of such a place, any more than one might alter a suit of chain mail by topping it with a Panama hat.

In such towns are businesses—shops and services—which live as the unassailable town lives, that is to say, in their own way and forever. Purveyors of the same shoes, sheets and sundries as the multicelled merchandizing mammoths sell go by the board, quite deserving of all that their critics say of them, that they can't keep up with the times, that they're dead and now must lie down. Defiance of time, of change, of anything is, after all, only defiance, and does not in itself guarantee a victory. But certain businesses, by their very nature, may be in a town, may *be* a town and achieve this defiant immortality. Anyone who has reflected with enough detachment on recent history is in a position to realize that, in revolutionary days, there must have been a certain market for genuine antiques made in America of American materials more than a century earlier. No technology advancing or static can eliminate the window-washer, the launderer, the handyman-smith and their establishments. Fashions in invention might change the vestments of their activity, but never their blood and marrow. The boat-wright becomes a specialist in wooden station-wagon bodies, and then in mobile-home interiors. The black-smith trades his leather bellows for a drill-press and a rack of epoxy resins, but he is what he was, and his shop is his permanence and his town's.

The general store has passed into the hands of the chains. It, and they, pursue the grail of *everything*, and since to be able to sell everything is on the face of it impossible, they are as impermanent as a military dictatorship that must expand or die, and that dies expanding. But there is another kind of store that sells, not everything, but *anything*. Its hallmark is that it has no grail at all, and therefore no pursuit. It emphatically does not expand. Its stock is that which has been useful or desirable to some people at some time; its only credo, that anything which has been useful or desirable to some people at some time will again be useful to someone—*anything*. Here you might find dried flowers under a glass dome, a hand-cranked coffee mill, a toy piano, a two-volume, leather-bound copy of *Dibdin's Journey,* a pair of two-wheel roller skates or a one tube radio set—the tube is a UX-11 and is missing—which tunes with a vario-coupler. You might—you probably would—also find in such a place a proprietor who could fix almost anything and has the tools to do it with, and who understands that conversation is important and the most important part of it is listening.

Such a town was North Nyack, New York, barely twenty miles from Manhattan, yet—but for superficial scratches—untouched and unchangeable. It contained such a business, the Anything Shoppe—a title that constituted one of the scratches, being a concession to the transient trade, but one that did not bleed— and such a proprietor. His name was Noat, George Noat. G-Note, naturally, to his friends, who were all the people who knew him. He was the ugliest man in town, but that, like the silliness of his concern's name, was only skin-deep.

Why such a trade should be his, or why he was its, might make for some interesting discussion of cause and effect. The fact—which would contribute nothing to the discussion—remained that there was an *anythingness* about G-Note; not only would he buy anything, sell anything or fix anything, he would also listen to anyone, help anyone and, from the depths of a truly extraordinary well of the quality called empathy—the ability to feel with another's fingertips, look out through another pair of eyes—he could understand.

To George Noat, Prop., then, at twenty minutes to three one stormy morning, came Gorwing.

"G-Note!" Gorwing roared, pounding on the front door of the Anything Shoppe with force enough to set adance the two sets of pony harness and the cabbage grater that hung against it. "G-Note, Goddammit!"

A dim light appeared in the back of the shop, and

G-Note's grotesque face and one T-shirted shoulder, over which a big square hand was pulling a gallus-strap, appeared at the edge of the baize curtain that separated G-Note's working from G-Note's living— the most partial of barriers, which suited him. He called, "It's open!" semaphored and withdrew.

Gorwing, small, quick, black hair, snapping black voice and eyes, sharp white teeth, slammed into the shop. The vibration set a clothing-dummy, atop which was perched a rubber imp carnival mask, teetering, and it turned as it teetered, bearing round on Gorwing indignantly. He and it stared one another in the eye for an angry moment, and then he cursed and snatched off the head and threw it behind the counter. "G-Note!" he barked.

G-Note shuffled into the shop, shrugging into a shawl-like grey cardigan and, with his heavy lids, wringing sleep out of his eyes. "I got that toilet you wanted yesterday," he mumbled. "Real tall, with pink rosebuds on. I bet there wouldn't be another like it from here to—"

"The hell with it," said Gorwing. "That was yesterday. Come *on*, willya?"

G-Note blinked at him. "Come?"

"The car, in the car!" Gorwing half cried, in the tones of excessive annoyance applied usually to people who should know by now. It was unfair, because by now G-Note did *not* know. "Hurry *up*, willya? What do I hafta do to make you hurry *up*?"

Gorwing flung open the door, and G-Note peered out into sodden blowing black. "It's raining out."

Gorwing's tight lips emitted a single sibilant explosion, and he raced out, leaving the door open. A moment later there came the sound of a car door slamming. G-Note shrugged and followed, closing the door behind him, and, hunching his shoulders against the driving rain, made his way out to the car. Gorwing had started it and switched on the lights while he was negotiating the puddles, then flung open the door on the driver's side and slid over into the passenger's seat. He shouted something.

"Huh?" G-Note grunted as he came poking and dripping into the car.

"I said Essex Street and Storms Road, right by the traffic light, and get *goin'*, willya?"

G-Note got himself settled and got going. "Gosh, Gorwing," he said, protesting gently.

"Quitcher bitchin'," said Gorwing through clamped teeth and curled lips. "Tromp down on that thing."

"Where we goin'?"

"I told you."

"Yeah, but—"

"You'll see when we get there. There's some money in it. You think I'd come out on a night like this if there wasn't some money in it? Listen, G-Note—" He paused with a mechanical abruptness, as if the machine gun with which he fired his words had jammed.

"What?"

Unjammed as suddenly, Gorwing shot: "You wouldn't let me down."

"No, I won't do that, but I wish I knew what I was 'sposed to do."

They sloshed over the high crown of Storms Hill and down the winding slope on the other side. The slick blacktop showed the loom of lights ahead before they saw the lights themselves—gold tinged with green, suddenly with ruby; the intersection and the traffic signal.

"Cut him out. *Quick!* Don't let'm pick up that guy."

Peering ahead, G-Note saw a car slowing for a waving figure who stood at the far side of the intersection. G-Note seemed not to have heard Gorwing's crackling order, or to have understood; yet it was as if his hands and feet had. The car lurched forward, cut in to the curb at the right of the other, and almost alongside. Startled, the other driver shifted and pulled away up the hill. At Gorwing's grunted order, G-Note stopped at the curb by the sodden and obviously bewildered pedestrian who had been trying to flag the other car. The man bent and tried to peer into the dark interior. Gorwing rolled down his window.

The man said, "Can you give me a lift?"

Gorwing reached back and opened the rear door, and the man plunged in. "Thank God," he panted, slamming the door. "I've got to get home, but I mean quick. You going near Rockland Lake?"

"We're going anywhere you say, mister," said Gorwing. "But it'll cost."

"Oh, that's all right. You're a taxi, hm?"

"We are now." Gorwing's hard hand took G-Note's elbow, squeezed, warned; but, warning or no, G-Note gasped at what came next: "Rockland Lake costs one hundred bucks from here."

G-Note's gasp was quite lost in the newcomer's wordless and indignant sound.

"What's the matter," Gorwing rasped, "can't raise it?"

"What kind of a holdup is this?" squeaked the man.

For the second time Gorwing reached back and swung the rear door open. Then he stretched across G-Note and shut off the motor. In the sudden silence, the sluicing of rain across the roof and the passenger's angry breath seemed too loud. Gorwing said, at a quarter the volume and twice the rasp, "I don't much go for that holdup talk."

The man plunged up and out—half out. He stood, with one foot still in the car, and looked up the road and down the road. Nothing moved but the rain. Clearly, they heard the relay in the traffic light saying *clock, chuck!* as the dim sodden shine of the intersection turned from green to red. To anyone thinking of traffic and transport, it was a persuasive sight. At three in the morning, chances of anything passing before daylight were remote.

He put his head back in. "Look, whoever you are, I've just *got* to get to Rockland Lake."

"So by now," said Gorwing, "we would be past Hook Mountain Road more'n halfway there. But you want to talk."

The man made his inarticulate sound and got back in. "Go ahead."

Gorwing, with a touch, checked G-Note's move toward the ignition. "A hundred bucks?"

"*Yes,* damn you!"

Gorwing turned the dome light on. "Take a good careful look at him," he said. Since he might have said it to either of them, they necessarily looked at one another, G-Note twisting around in his seat to look back, the passenger huddled sullen and glaring in the rear corner. G-Note saw a soft-handed petulant man in his early thirties, with very fine, rather receding reddish hair and surprisingly bright blue eyes.

G-Note's great ugly head loomed over him like an approaching rockfall. The domelight, almost directly overhead, accentuated the heavy ridges of bone over his eyes, leaving the eyes themselves all but invisible in their caves. It gleamed from the strong fleshy arches that walled his wide nostrils and conceal the soft sensitivity of his thin upper lip while making the most of the muscular protruding underlip.

"You'll pay," said Gorwing, grinning wolfishly and switching off the light. "Drive," he said, nudging G-Note. He laughed. "I got a witness and you ain't," he said cheerfully.

"Just hurry," said the passenger.

G-Note, wondering more than anything else at the first laugh he had ever heard from Gorwing, drove. He said, unhappily, "This ain't a fun one, this time."

"Shut up," Gorwing said.

"Can't you go any faster?" cried the passenger.

He got no response. Only the anxious would feel that this skilled hurtling was not fast enough. No object, including an automobile, was inanimate with G-Note's big hands upon it; this one moved as if it knew its own way and its own weight.

"In here," said the passenger.

"I always wondered," said Gorwing. His meaning was clear. Many must have wondered just who lived behind these stone posts, these arresting NO ADMITTANCE and PRIVATE ROAD, KEEP OUT and NO TURNING and DEAD END ROAD signs. The drive climbed, turning, and in fifty yards one would have thought the arterial road below had ceased to exist. They came to a T. Neat little signs with arrows said SMITH on the left and POLLARD on the right. "Left," said the passenger.

They climbed again, and abruptly the road was manicured, rolled, tended, neat. "This will do."

There was a turn-around; the drive continued, apparently to a garage somewhere. In the howling wet, there was the shadowed white mass of a house. The man opened the door.

"A hundred bucks," Gorwing said.

The man took out his wallet. Gorwing turned on the dome light.

"I have only twenty here. Twenty-one."

"You got it inside." It could have been a question.

"*Damn* it!" the man flared. "Four lousy miles!"

"You was in a awful hurry," Gorwing drawled. He took the twenty, and the one, out of the man's hand. "I want the rest of it."

The man got out of the car and backed off into the rain. From about forty feet, he shrieked at them. He meant, undoubtedly, to roar like a lion, but his voice broke and he shrieked. "Well, I won't pay it!" and then he ran like a rabbit.

"Yes you will!" Gorwing bellowed. He slammed the back door of the car, which, if heard by the fleeing man, must have doubled his speed.

"Don't go out in that," said G-Note.

"Oh, I ain't about to," said Gorwing. "He'll pay in the morning. He'll pay you."

"Me?"

"You drop me off home and then come back and park here," said Gorwing. "Don't for Pete's sake go back to bed. You want to sleep any more, you do it right here. When he sees you he'll pay. You won't have to say nothing. Just be here."

G-Note started the car and backed, turning. "Oh, why not just let it go? You got more than it's worth."

Gorwing made a laughing noise. This was not the laugh that had amazed G-Note before; it was the one that G-Note had thought was all the laughter Gorwing had. It was also all the answer Gorwing would offer.

G-Note said, sadly, "You *like* doing this to that fellow."

Gorwing glanced at the road-signs as they pulled

out of the driveway. "Private Road," he read aloud, but not very. It was as if to say, "He can afford it."

"Well," said G-Note again, as they neared North Nyack, "This ain't a fun one, this time."

There had been "fun ones." Like the afternoon Gorwing had come roaring and snapping into his place, just as urgently as he had tonight, demanding to know if G-Note had a copy of *Trials and Triumphs, My Forty Years in The Show Business,* by P. T. Barnum; and G-Note had! And they had tumbled it, with a lot of other old books, into two boxes, and had driven out to the end of Carrio Lane, where Gorwing just knew there was somebody who needed the book—not who, not why, just that there was somebody who needed it—and he and G-Note had stood at opposite sides of the lane, each with a box of books, and had bellowed at each other, "You got the P. T. Barnum book over there?" and "I don't know if I have the P. T. Barnum book here; have you got the P. T. Barnum book there?" and "What is the name of the P. T. Barnum book?" and *"Trials and Triumphs, My Forty Years in The Show Business,"* and so on, until, sure enough, a window popped open and a lady called down, "Do one of you men really have Barnum's biography there?" and, when they said they had, she said it was a miracle; she came down and gave them fifteen dollars for it. And that other time, when at Gorwing's urgent behest, G-Note had gone on a hot summer's day to stand blinking in the sun at Broad and Main streets, with a heavy ancient hand-cranked music box unwrapped on his shoulder, and the city man had come running up to him to ask what it played: *"Skater's Waltz,"* G-Note had told him, "and *My Rosary."* "I'll give you a hundred bucks for it," the man had said, and, when G-Note's jaw dropped and fumbled for an astonished word, he'd made it a hundred and a quarter and had paid it, then and there.

Fun ones, these and others, and it hadn't mattered that the customers (or was it victims?) paid exorbitantly. They did it of their own free will, and they seemed really to *need* whatever it was. How Gorwing knew what was needed, and where—but never by whom or why—was a recurrent mystery; but after a while you stopped asking—because Gorwing wouldn't stand catechizing on the subject—and then you stopped wondering; you just went along with it, the way you do with automatic shifting, the innards of an IBM machine, or, if you happen not to know, precisely what chemicals are put into the head of a match to make it light. You don't *have* to know.

But this man, this passenger they'd charged twenty-five dollars per mile now; it wasn't fun. He was a guy in trouble if ever G-Note had seen one, anxious, worried, even frantic—so anxious he'd say yes to a demand like that, even if he did take it back later; so anxious he was stumbling homeward through the rain at three in the morning. You should help a fellow like that, you shouldn't use his trouble against him. Which didn't seem to bother Gorwing, not one bit: coming into the street-lit area of North Nyack, now, G-Note could glance sidewise at Gorwing's face, see the half grin, the cruel white teeth showing. No, it didn't bother Gorwing.

So . . . you found out new things about people all the time. Such a thing could be surprising, but, if you don't want surprises like that, you just keep away from people. Thus G-Note shrugged away the matter, as he asked, "Where you staying now?" for Gorwing moved around all the time.

"Just drop me off by O'Grady's."

O'Grady's, the poolhall, was across town from G-Note's place, on the same avenue; yet, passing his own shop, G-Note turned right and made the usual wide detour past the hospital. He made a U-turn at the poolhall and stopped. For a good-night, Gorwing had only, "Now you said you wouldn't let me down."

"All right," said G-Note.

"Forty-sixty, you and me," said Gorwing, and turned away.

G-Note drove off.

Eloise Smith hoped Jody wouldn't be mad. His was not the towering rage of this one nor the sullen grumps of that one, but a waspish, petty, verbose kind of anger, which she had neither the wit nor the words to cope with. She loved Jody and tried her very best to have everything the way he wanted it, but it was hard, sometimes, to know what would annoy him. And when anything did, sometimes she had to go through an hour or more of his darting, flicking admonishments before she even knew what it was.

She'd broken the telephone. Kicked the wire right out of the wall—oh, how *clumsy*! But she'd done worse than that from time to time, and he'd just laughed. Or she'd done much less serious things and he'd carried on just terrible. Well . . . she'd just have to wait and see. She hoped she could stay awake, waiting —goodness, he was late. Elks nights were always the latest; he was secretary, and was always left to lock the hall after the meeting. But he usually got home by two anyway—it was three already, and still no sign of—oh—*there* he . . .

She ran and opened the door. He spun in, dripping,

out of breath. He slammed the door and shot the bolt, and pushed past her to peer out the front window. Not that anything could be seen out there. He turned from the window. He looked wild. She stood before him, clutching her negligee against her breast.

"Eloise . . . you all right?"

"All right? Why, of course I'm all right!"

"Thank God!" He pushed past her again, darted to the living room door, flicked his gaze across and back. "You all alone?"

"Well, not since you got here," she said, in a hopeless attempt to produce some levity. "Here, you're wet through. Give me your hat. You poor—"

"It might interest you to know . . . you've driven me half out . . . of my mind," he panted. She had never seen him like this. He might be a little short of breath from running from the car to the house, but not this much, and it should be, well, tapering off. It wasn't. It seemed to get more marked as he talked. He was very pale. His red-rimmed eyes and the rain running off his bland features gave him the ludicrous expression of a five-year-old who has bumped his head and is trying not to cry. She followed him into the living room and rounded on him, to face him, and for the third time he pushed past her, this time to fling open the dining room door. She said timidly, "Jody, I broke the telephone. I mean, I fell over the wire and it came out."

"Oh, you did, did you."

He was still panting. "Jody!" she cried, "whatever is the *matter*? What's *happened*?"

"Oh, what's happened?" he barked. His eyes were too round. "I call you up and somebody cuts the wire, as far as I know. I rush out of the hall to the car and the door slams behind me, that's all. My keys on the table. Can't get back in, can't start the car. Try my best to get here quickly. Hitchhiking. Get waylaid by a couple of the ugliest hoodlums you ever saw, they *robbed* me."

'Oh dear—did they hurt you, honey?"

'They did not. Matter of fact," he panted, "I told them off, but good. And they better not fool with me again. Not that they will—I guess they learned their lesson." Angrily, proudly, he hitched his shoulders, a gesture that made him aware of his wet coat, which at last he began to remove. She ran to help him. "Oh Jody, Jody darling, but you didn't have to rush back like that . . ."

"Didn't I," he said solemnly, in a tone dripping with meaning, not one whit of which she understood. He pulled himself, glaring, away from her, and, while she stood clutching her negligee to herself again, he ponderously took off the coat, glaring at her.

"Oh, I'm *so* sorry. You poor dear." She thought, suddenly, of a woman she had seen in the parking lot at the supermarket, whose child had bolted in front of a car. People had shrieked, brakes had squealed, the woman had run out to scoop up her frightened but unharmed youngster—and, in her relief, had whaled the tar out of him.

That was it—Jody had been so terribly worried about her, he'd gotten into all this trouble rushing to help her, and now that he knew she was safe he was, in effect, spanking her.

She grew very tender, very patient. "Oh *Jody* . . ." she said fondly.

"You won't 'Oh Jody' out of this one," he said.

"Well, I'm *sorry!*" she cried, and, "Oh, Jody, what is it? Is it the telephone? Will it be hard to get it fixed?"

"The *telephone* can be fixed," he growled in a voice again inexplicably loaded with meaning. He passed through the dining room into the kitchen, again flicking his glance here, there, up, across. "Got everything put away," he said, looking at the glass cupboard, the dish shelf.

"Well, don't I always?"

"Doubtless," he said bitterly. He opened the refrigerator.

"Let me fix—"

"I'll do it myself," he said.

Her tenderness and patience gave out at that point. She said in a small voice, "I'll go to bed then," and when he did not respond, she went upstairs, lay down and cried.

She managed to be silent, stiff and silent, when he came upstairs, and lay in the dark with her eyes squeezed shut while he undressed and washed and got into his pajamas and into the other bed. She deeply hoped he'd stay something, but he didn't. After a long time, she whispered, "Well, good night, Jody." He made a sound which might have been an offensive "Ha!" or just a grunt; she couldn't be sure. She thought he fell asleep after a while, and then she did, too—lightly, troubled.

The glare of her bed lamp awoke her. Up through it, and up through the confusion of puzzlement and sleepiness, she blinked at Jody. Seen so, standing by her bed and glaring down at her, he looked very large. He never had before.

He said, "You'd better tell me all about it right now."

She said, "Wh-what time is it?"

"Now you listen to me, Eloise. I've learned a whole lot of things in the last few hours. About you. About me. About—" Suddenly he raised his voice, at the rim of the glare of light, the vein at the side of his neck swelled. "I'm just too doggoned nice to everybody. When I told off those thugs, I tell you, something happened to me, and from now on I won't stand for it any more!"

"Jody—"

"Two of them, twice my size, and I told *them*."

"You did?"

In retrospect, Eloise was to look painfully back upon this moment and realize that on it turned everything that subsequently happened between them; she would realize that when she said, "You *did*?" he heard "*You* did?"—a difference in inflection that becomes less subtle the more one thinks about it. Later, she thought a great deal about it; now, however, she could only shrink numbly down into the covers as he roared, "Yes, *I* did! You didn't think I had it in me, did you? Well I did, and from now on nobody puts anything over on me! Including you, you hear?"

"But Jody—I—"

"Who was here when I called you up at two o'clock?"

"Who was— *No*body!"

He sank down to the edge of his bed so their heads were more nearly on a level, and fixed her with a pink-rimmed, weepy, steely gaze. "I . . . heard . . . you," he intoned.

"You mean when you called?"

He simply sat there with his unchanging, unnatural glare. Wonderingly, frightened, she shook her head. "I was watching a movie on TV. It was just ending— the very end; it was a good one. And I—I—"

"You told your . . . your . . ." He could not say the word. "You told whoever it was not to talk. *But I heard you.*"

Dazedly she sat up in bed, a slim, large-eyed, dark-blonde woman in her late twenties—frightened, deeply puzzled, warding off certain hurt. She thought hard, and said, "I spoke to *you*—I said that to you! In the picture, you see, there was this girl that . . . that . . . Oh, never mind; it's just that in that last moment of the picture everything came together, like. And just as you rang and I picked up the phone, it was the last minute of the picture, don't you see? I was sort of into it—you know. So I said to you, 'Don't say anything for a second, honey,' and I— Is *that* what you heard?"

"That is what I heard," he said coldly.

She laughed with relief. "I said it to you, to you, not to anyone here, you silly! And—well, I was sort of mixed up, coming out of the TV that way, to the phone, and you began to sort of shout at me, and I couldn't hear the TV, and I kind of ran to it to turn it up, just for a second, and I forgot I was holding the phone and the wire caught my ankle and I fell down and the wire pulled out and—*Jody!*" she cried, seeing his face.

"You're a liar, you bitch."

"Jody!" she whispered faintly. Slowly she lay down again. She closed her eyes, and tears crept from beneath her lids. She made no sound.

"I can handle hoodlums and I can handle you," he said flatly, and turned out the light. 'And from now on," he added, as if it were a complete statement; he must have thought so, for he said nothing more that night.

Eloise Smith lay trembling, her mind assuring her over and over that none of this was really happening, it couldn't happen. After a useless time of that, she began to piece the thing together, what he'd said, what she'd said . . . she recalled suddenly what he had blurted out about the Elks' Hall, and the car, and all . . . what was it? Oh: he'd called, apparently to tell her he was on the way; and she'd murmured, "Don't say anything for a second, honey," and he'd thought . . . he must have thought oh dear, how *silly* of him! "Jody!" she said, sitting up, and then the sight of his dim rigid form, curled away from her in the other bed, drove her back to silence, and she lay down to think it through some more. . . . And he'd gotten himself all upset and yelled, and then she'd broken the wire, and probably thought her—*her* —but she could not think the word any more than he had been able to say it—he'd thought that whoever it was had gaily pulled out the wire to, well, stop his interruption. And then apparently Jody had gone all panicky and berserk, had run straight out to the car, got himself locked out of the Elks' Hall with the car keys still inside, had headed north—away from town, and gas stations, and other telephones—and had tried to hitchhike home. And something about hood-lums and being robbed on the way—but then he said he'd driven them off, didn't he?

She gave it up at length. Whatever had happened to him, he obviously felt like a giant, or a giant-killer maybe, for the first time in his life, and he was taking it out on her.

Well, maybe in the morning—

In the morning he was even worse. He hardly spoke to her at all. Just watched her every minute, and once in a while snorted disgustedly. Eloise moved quickly with poached egg, muffin, coffee, marmalade; sleep-less, shaken, she would know what to do, take a stand, have a sensible thought, even—later; not now.

Watching her, Jody wiped his lips, threw down his napkin and stood up. "I'm going for the car. If you're thinking of letting anybody in, well, look out, that's all. You don't know when I'll be back."

"Jody, Jody!" she wailed, "I never! I *never,* Jody!"

He walked past her, smiling tightly, and got his other hat. "Oh boy," he said to the cosmos, "I just hope I run across one of those thugs again, that's what I hope." He banged the hat with the edge of his hand, and set it uncharacteristically at a rakish slant on his head. Numbly, she followed him to the door and stood in it, watching him go. He sprang up the steep driveway like a spring lamb. At the top he turned without breaking stride and came straight back—but not springing—scuttling would be the word for it. His face was chalky. He saw her and tried, with some apparent difficulty, to regain his swagger. "Forgot to call the phone company. Get a taxi, too."

"You can't," she said. "I broke the wire."

"I know, I know!" he snapped waspishly, though she felt he had forgotten it. "I'll call from Pollard's." He glanced quickly over his shoulder, up the driveway, and then plunged across the lawn and through the wet shrubbery toward their only neighbor's home.

She looked after him in amazement, and then up the drive. Over its crest, she could see the roof of a car, obviously parked in their turnaround. She was curious, but too much was happening; she would not dare climb the drive to see who it was. Instead went in and closed the door and climbed upstairs, where she could see from the bedroom windows. From this elevation the car was plainly visible. It wasn't theirs. Also visible was the ugly giant lounging tiredly against the car, watching the house.

She shrank behind the curtain and put all her left fingers in her mouth.

After a time she saw Jody plunging across the

long grass of the vacant acre that lay between their place and Pollard's. He pushed through the shrubs at the edge of the lawn, stopped to paddle uselessly at his damp trouser-legs and then sidled over to the driveway. He peeped around the hollyhocks until he could look up the drive. The ugly man had apparently detected some movement, for he stood up straight and peered. Jody shrank back behind the hollyhocks.

She thought then that he might come in, but instead he crouched there. There was a long—to Eloise, an interminable—wait. Then a taxi pulled in from the road and turned to stop next to the other car. Jody straightened up and began trotting up the drive. The ugly man leaned his elbows on the lower edge of the taxi driver's window—he had to bend nearly double to do it—and began speaking to him. Of course she could not hear a word, but the ugly man and the driver seemed to be laughing. Then the ugly man reached in, slapped the driver cheerfully on the shoulder and stood back. The taxi started up, backed around and pulled out of the drive. Jody, seeing this, for the second time made a U-turn and scuttled back to his hiding place behind the hollyhocks. He looked very little like a man who was overanxious to meet some thugs.

Eloise moved closer to the window in order to see him better, for he was almost straight down beneath her. Perhaps he caught the movement out of the corner of his eye, or perhaps some sixth sense . . . anyway, he glanced up, and for a moment looked more miserable than a human being ought, caught like that—chagrined, embarrassed. Then, visibly, he began to grow angry again; it began with her, she could see that. Then he wheeled and marched up the drive like a condemned man ascending the scaffold. The ugly man opened the right front door of his old sedan, and Jody got in.

For a long time Eloise Smith stood in the window, kneading her elbows and frowning. Then, slowly, she went downstairs and began to write a letter.

Smith's posture of pugnacious defiance lasted from the turnaround to the private road he shared with Pollard. Once out of sight of the house, he slumped unhappily into the corner of his seat and stole a quick glance at his captor.

The man was even bigger, and considerably uglier, in daylight than he had been in the dark. He said, "I sent away your taxi. He didn't mind. He's an old buddy of mine."

"Oh," said Jody.

He watched the scenery go by, and thought of how gentle the man's voice was. Very soft and gentle. Into this Jody Smith built vast menace. After a while he said sulkily, "This going to cost me another hundred?"

"Oh gosh no," said the ugly man. "You bought a round trip. Where do you want to go?"

Cat-and-mouse, thought Jody. Trying to get my goat. "Got to get my car at the Elks' Hall."

"Okay," the man said, nodding pleasantly. Deftly, he spun the wheel, turning into what Smith prided himself as being *his* short cut to the Hall. Obviously this creature knew the roads hereabouts.

They came to the built-up area, slid into an alley, crossed two streets and turned sharp right into the crunchy parking yard at the Elks. There were two other cars there, one Smith's the other obviously the caretaker's, for the doors stood open and the old man was sweeping the step.

Timidly, Smith touched the door handle. The ugly man sat still, big gnarled hands on the wheel, eyes straight ahead. Smith opened the door and said, ". . . well—" Then, incredulous, he got out. The ugly man made no attempt to stop him.

Smith actually got two paces away from the car before sheer compulsive curiosity got the better of him. He went back and said, "Look, what about this money? You don't really expect me to pay a hundred dollars for that ride."

"I don't," said the big man, "Gorwing, I guess he does."

"Gorwing. Is that the little ape that—"

"He's a friend of mine," said the giant, not loudly, but just quickly. Smith dropped that tactic, and asked, "You work for him?"

"With, not for. Sometimes."

"But you're doing the collecting."

"Look," said the ugly one, suddenly, "Gorwing, he wants sixty percent of that money. Well, I wouldn't let him down. For me, I don't want it. Now, how much did he get off you last night?"

"Twenty-one."

"From sixty is thirty-nine. You got thirty-nine bucks?"

"Not on me." Astonished, he looked at the grotesque face. "Tell me something. What would you do if I wouldn't give you another penny?"

The man looked at his gnarled hands, which twisted on the wheel. "I guess I'd just have to put it up myself."

Smith got back in. "Run me over to the bank."

The man made no comment, but started his engine.

"What's your name?" asked Smith as they stopped for a light a block away.

"George Noat."

"Aren't you afraid I'll go to the police?"

"Nope."

Smith recalled then, forcefully, what Gorwing had said: "I got a witness and you haven't." He imagined himself trying to explain what had happened to a desk sergeant, who would be trying to write it all down in a book. Outrageous, certainly—but he had gotten into the car of his own free will, he had agreed to pay.

"How did you happen to come along when you did last night?"

"Just driving by."

Smith found the answer unsatisfying, and he could not say why. He said, sulkily, "Friend or not, I've got to say that your Gorwing is a bandit."

"No he ain't," said George Noat mildly. "Not when all he does is get things people really need. You really need something, you pay for it, right?"

"Yes, I suppose you—"

"And if you need something, and a fellow delivers it, nobody's getting robbed."

At that moment they came to the bank, and the subject was lost.

Jody Smith lived with the letter for a long time.

Dear Jody,

After the way you acted last night I don't know what to do except I have to go away from you. You have to trust a person. I always believed you but why did you make up all that about Mr. Noat I know him a long time and he is about the

kindest man who ever lived he wouldn't hurt a
fly.

I want you to think about one thing you said
a lot about me and some man and all that, well I
want you to know that there isn't any man at all
and now that means your wife left you and there
wasn't even any other man. I bet now you wish
there was. I wish there was. No I don't Jody,
oh my goodness I wish I could write a letter I
never could you know, but I can't stay here any
more. Maybe you could find somebody better I
guess you better I won't stand in your way because I still want you to be happy.

Eloise

Tell the market not to send the order I sent yesterday. We were supposed to have dinner at the
Stewarts Tuesday. I can't think of anything else.

Now Jodham Swaine Smith was a man of independent means—this was the phrase with which on
occasion he described himself to himself. His parents
had both come from well-to-do families, but Smith
was two generations—three, on his mother's side—removed from the kind of fortune-getting that had gotten these fortunes; latterly, it had become the Smith
tradition to treat the principal as if it did not exist,
and live modestly on the interest.

Independent means. Such independence means all
Four Freedoms plus a good many more. Small prep
schools—in small towns and with, comparatively, small
fees—gray as Groton, followed by tiny, honored col-
leges on which the ivy, if not the patina, is quite as
real as Harvard's, make it possible to grow up in one
of the most awesome independencies of all, the free-

dom from Life. In most cases it takes but six or so post-
graduate weeks for trauma and tragedy to set in, and
for the discoveries to be made that business is not
necessarily conducted on the honor system, that the
reward for dutifully reporting the errors of the erring
gets you, not a mark toward your Good Citizen But-
ton, but something more like a kick in the teeth, and
finally, that the world is full of people who never
heard of your family and wouldn't give a damn if they
had.

Yet for those few who are enabled by, on the one
hand, the effortless accumulation of dividends, and
on the other, an absence of personal talent or am-
bition that might be challenged, it is possible to slip
into a surrogate of man's estate in its subjective aspects
hardly different from the weatherproof confines of
the exclusive neighborhood, the private school and
the honored and unheard-of college. Jody Smith was
one of these few.

Not that he didn't face the world, just as squarely
and as valiantly as he had been taught to do. But it
happened that, all unknowing, he gave the world nothing worth abrading, and the world was therefore, as
far as he could know, a smooth place to live with. In
no sense did he withdraw from life. On the contrary,
he sought out the centers of motion, and involved
himself as completely as possible with the Elks, the
Rotary, the Lions, and the Civic Improvement League.
Strangely enough, these gatherings, filled as they
were with real people, gave him no evidence of the
existence of a real world. Jody Smith was always
available for the Thanksgiving Dance Committee and
Operation Santa Claus, but did not submit himself
and was somehow never proposed, for any chairman-
ship. In a word, he wasn't competition for anyone.

And he had gravitated to that same strange other—
or no—world in what might laughingly be called his
business. He was a philatelist. He ran small classified
advertisements in the do-it-yourself and other mag-
azines on a contract basis, and handled the trickle of
mail from his little den at home. He made money at
it. He also lost money at it. In the aggregate, he probably lost more than he made, but not enough to
jeopardize his small but adequate and utterly pre-
dictable income.

He had, from time to time, wanted this or that. He
had never for a moment *needed* anything. Eloise, for
example—he had wanted her, or perhaps it was to be
married to her, but he hadn't needed to. She helped
him with his business, typing out some of the cor-
respondence from form letters he had composed, and
moistening stamp hinges. But he did not need her
help. He did not need her.

Not even when she left. For a while. Weeks, in
fact. And even then at first it was want, not need, and
even then the want was to create some circumstance
that would make her realize how wrong she had been.
Then the wants widened, somehow. The television
and the stamp hinges seemed after a time to be in-
adequate to fill the long evenings or to occupy the
silence of the house. When no hand but his own
moved anything about him, his hat would not go of
itself into the closet but remained on hall tables
where he himself had put it. And, where at first he
had rather admired himself for his cookery, for he
was a methodical, meticulous, and, as far as cook-
books were concerned, obedient person, he began
slowly to resent the kitchen and even the animal
beneath his belt which with such implacability drove
him into it. It seemed to him a double burden—that

he should have to put in all that time before a meal, and then have nothing ready until he prepared it himself. To do things in order to make lunchtime come seemed ultimately enough, more than enough, for a man to be burdened with. Then to have to do things to make the lunch itself seemed an intolerable injustice.

These matters of convenience—and lack of it—grew into nuisances and then, like the pebble in the shoe, like the inability to turn over even in the most comfortable of beds, into sheer torture.

The breaking point came, oddly enough, not in the long night hours with the empty bed beside his, nor in some dream-wracked and disoriented morning, but in the middle of an otherwise pleasant afternoon. He had just received the new Scott's catalog, and wanted to compare something in it with the 1954 edition. He couldn't find the 1954 edition, and he called out:

"Eloise—"

The sound of his own voice, and of her name, made something happen like the tearing of a membrane. It tore so completely, and with such suddenness and agony, that he grunted aloud and fell back on the couch. He sat there for a moment weaving, and his mouth grew crooked and his eyes pink, and there came a warning sting at the very back of the roof of his mouth that astonishingly informed him, as it hardly had since he was nine years old, that he was about to cry.

He didn't cry, beyond once whimpering, "Eloise?" in a soprano half-whisper; then for a long time he sat silent and stunned, wondering numbly how such a force could have remained coiled so tightly within him, undetected.

When he could, he began to take stock. It was a matter of weeks—six of them, seven—since she had left, and not once had he examined his acts and attitude. He had done nothing about locating her, though in that department there was little to be done —he simply did not know where she was. Her only relative was an aging mother in a rest home out West, and she certainly had not gone there. He had not destroyed her letter, but he hadn't reread it either, nor thought about its contents. He hadn't wanted to think about these things, he now knew. He had thought . . . he hadn't *needed* to.

He needed to now, and he did. The letter gave him nothing at first but a feeling—not quite anger—more like a sullen distaste for himself. And one more thing, slightest of handholds—she apparently, somehow or other, knew George Noat.

And, on that slender evidence, he tore out of the house and got into his car.

Nothing was the way it should be. The trail was not obscure. The taxi-driver—Noat had said he was "an old buddy"—told him immediately where Noat and his business were, and there were no obstacles to his finding the place—it was within three blocks of the Elks' Hall. The fact that never once in Elks or Lions or Rotary had he heard Noat's name was only surprising, not mysterious: such establishments as the Anything Shoppe look back, not forward, and are not found on the lists of forward-looking organizations.

It was only in the subdued light of the shop (pe) , with the oldfashioned spring-swung doorbell still jangling behind him, that Jodham Swaine Smith realized that, though intuition and evidence had brought him here, they had not supplied him with the right thing to say. "Mr. Noat!" he bleated urgently, and then dried up altogether.

The proprietor glanced up at him from his work, and said easily, "Oh, hi. Give a hand here, will you?"

Annoyed, which was uncharacteristic of him, and simultaneously much more timid than he ever remembered being, Jody Smith edged around the counter. Noat was squatting before an inverted kitchen chair, painted flat red, with a broken spoke and a split seat-board. "Just grab holt here," he invited. Smith took the legs as indicated and squeezed them together, while Noat drove in corrugated fasteners. "Nothing wrong with the chair," said Noat philosophically between hammer blows. "It's people. People busted this chair. As for fixing it, if people had sense enough to have four arms like this thing has four legs, why, I wouldn't have to call on my neighbors. You like people?"

The direct question startled Smith; he had been about to interrupt, and was only half following what the big man said. He made a weak uncertain laugh, very like that of Sir Laurence in the Graveyard Scene, and said, "Sure. Sure I do."

He stood back while Noat turned the chair upright, set it on the counter and measured the missing spoke with an ancient and frayed dressmaker's tape. "You got to make allowances," Noat said to the tape. "This old thing's stretched, but you see I know just how much it's stretched. 14 inches here is 14 and 17/32nds actual. That's one way to make allowances. Then," he went on, laying the tape against a piece of square stock that was chucked in a highly individual wood lathe, "if the tape says 14 on the chair, and I mark it the same 14 on the lumber, it comes out right and it makes no never mind *what* it is actual.

People," he said, rounding at last on Smith, who prepared himself for some profound truth, "fret too much."

Smith lived for a moment with that feeling one has when mounting ten steps in the dark, then discovers there are only nine stairs. He grasped wildly at what he thought the man had been talking about. "People are all right. I mean, I like people."

Noat considered this, or a turning chisel he had obviously made from an old screwdriver, carefully. Smith could not stand the contemplative silence, and ran on. "Why, I do everything for people. I join every club or lodge in town that does any good for people, and I work hard at it. I guess I wouldn't do that if I didn't like people."

"You don't do that for yourself." It was, if a statement, agreement and a compliment; if a question, a searching, even embarrassing one, calling for more insight than Smith had or dared to have. It was voiced as a statement, but so nearly as a question that Smith could not be sure. He was, however, too honest a person to grasp at the compliment . . . and if he rejected it, he must be embarrassed, even insulted, and walk out. . . . but he couldn't walk out until he—"You know my wife, don't you?"

"Sure do. A very nice little lady."

He started the lathe. It made a very strange sound. The power looked like that from an ancient upright vacuum cleaner. Reduction was accomplished through gears that could only have come from one of those hand-operated coffee mills that used, with their great urn-shaped hoppers and scroll-spoked, cast-iron scarlet flywheels, to grace chain markets before they became supered. The frame was that of a treadle-operated sewing machine, complete with treadle, which, never having been disconnected, now disappeared in a blur of oscillation that transferred itself gently to everything in the place. One could not see it, but it was there in the soles of the feet, in the microscopic erection of the fibers in a dusty feather boa, in the way sun-captured dust motes marched instead of wandered. The lathe's spur-center seemed to have been the business end of a planing attachment from some forgotten drill press; it was chucked into a collett that seemed to have been handmade out of rock maple. The cup center, at the other end, turned freely and true in what could be nothing else but a roller-skate wheel. Noat set his ground-down screwdriver on the long tool rest, which was of a size and massiveness that bespoke a history of angle-bracketship aboard a hay wagon. On the white wood a whiter line appeared, and a blizzard of fragrant dust appeared over Noat's heavy wrists. He carried the tool along the rest, and the whiter-upon-white became a band, a sheet. When he had taken it from end to end, he stopped the machine. The wood was still square, but with all its corners rounded. Smith tore his fascinated eyes away from it and asked, wondering if Noat would still know what he was talking about, "How did you happen to know her?"

"Customer."

"Really?"

Noat squinted at the display window over the edge of his chisel. "Garlic press," he said, and pursed his lips. "Swedish cookie mold, by golly, she was here seven times over that. Little lady really gets two bits out of each two dozen pennies." He laughed quietly; he had a good laugh. Smith's solar plexus contained a sudden vacuum at the mention of these homey, Eloise-y things. "And the egg separators—two hundred egg separators."

"What? I never saw—"

"Yes, you did. You went away to some kind of convention, and when you came back she'd done over the breakfast nook."

"The textured wall!"

"Yeah, those mash-paper cushions they put between layers in an egg crate. She cut and fit and put 'em up and painted 'em—what she say?" He closed his eyes. "Flat purple with dull gold in the middle of each cup."

"She never told me," Smith informed himself aloud. "She said she'd . . . Well, I guess she didn't actually *say.* But I got the idea she saved up from the house money and had it done. She really did it herself?"

Noat nodded gravely.

"I wonder why she didn't tell me," Smith breathed.

"Maybe," said George Noat, "she thought you might live with a textured wall where you wouldn't with egg separators."

There was a meaning here that he could not—would not—see, but that he knew would come to him most distastefully later. He compressed his lips. He had acquired too many things to think about in the last few minutes, and at least two of them might be insults. He glanced doorward, and said in farewell tones, "Well, I—" and then the handle of the chisel pressed into his palm stopped him. "You go on with that. I got to cook some glue."

Smith stared with horror at the chisel. "Me run that machine? I never in my life—"

The giant cupped a hand under his left armpit

and propelled him to the machine. "The one wonderful thing about a lathe, you couldn't tell a beginner's first job from Chippendale's last one. Don't ever get all big-eyed over beautiful work—chances are it was real easy to do. What I always say is, Duncan Phyfe is only a piccoloful of whiskey."

"But—but—"

"Pull this chain, starts it. Rest your chisel here, cut light and slow at first. Anytime you want to see what you've done or feel it, pull the chain again, it stops. That's all there is." He started the machine, took the chisel, and, under its traveling point, the wood drew on a new garment of texture from end to end.

Timidly, Smith took back the chisel and nervously approached the spinning wood. It touched, and he sprang back, but there was a new neat ring around it. Fascinated, he tried it again, and again, and then looked up to ask if that was right: but Noat had confidently retired to the other end of the shop, where a disgraceful-looking glue pot sat upon a gas ring.

Nothing could have given him more assurance than to be trusted with the job like this. For a while, then, he entered the magical, never-quite-to-be-duplicated region of The First Time. You may challenge the world to find anyone who runs a lathe and who also forgets the first cut he ever made.

Disappointingly soon, the square wood was round; but then he realized joyfully that this would be a new spoke for the chair, and must come down quite a bit more. He worked steadily and carefully, until at last his mind was able to watch it while it thought of other things as well—and it thought of Eloise, thought of Eloise in a way unknown to it for oh . . . oh, a long time; and for such a brief while, too—there was some-

thing deeply sad about that. The day—no, two days—
before he had stumblingly asked her to marry him, he
had been in a drugstore, just like any other drugstore
except for the climactic fact that it was in her neighborhood, the one she always went to, *her* drugstore.
He had walked in to get some cough drops and had
suddenly realized this incredible thing about the place
—that she had many times stood here, had bent over
that showcase, had had that prim warm little body
cupped there by the padded swivel seats at the soda
fountain. She had smiled in this place. Her voice had
vibrated the sliding glass over the vitamins, and her
little feet must have lightly dotted the floor, from time
to time, just after it had been waxed.

And so it was with the Anything Shoppe; her hand
had danced the spring-dangling doorbell, and she had
bargained here and made plans, and counted money
and held it for a moment, while the three fine "thinking" furrows—two long and one short—came between
her eyebrows, and went quickly, leaving no mark. She
had smiled in this place, and perhaps laughed; and
here she had thought of him.

Textured wall.

The turning wood had grown silky, and now seemed
to be growing a sheath of mist . . . he withdrew the
tool and stood watching it through the blur until a
bulky rectangular object on the tool rest distracted
him. He blinked, and saw it was a box of tissues.
Gratefully he reached for one and blew his nose and
wiped his eyes. He gazed guiltily at Noat, but the big
man's back was turned and he appeared to be totally
absorbed in stirring his stinking glue. Let's not think
about how he put the tissues there, or why . . . turn off
the machine now.

George Noat found it not necessary to turn to him

until he spoke: "Getting a cold, I guess . . . sniff . . . time of year. Mr. Noat, have a look at this now."

Noat lumbered back to the lathe and ran his hand along the piece. His hands were those a prep-school boy might see from the windows of the school bus, that a collegian with a school letter on the front of his sweater might see manipulating the mysteries under a car. One seldom noticed the skill of such hands, but ingrained black was dirt and dirt was, vaguely, "them," not "us." The idea does cling, oh yes it does, ingrained, too. Yet for all his distress in this moment, Smith was able to notice how the great grainy leather-brown hand closed all around the stainless new wood, was intimate with it from end to end, left not a mark. To Smith it was an illumination, to see such a hand live so with purity. All this subliminal; still before his stinging eyes was the mist of hurting, and he said aloud, "She left me."

"That's just *fine*," said George Noat. He must have meant one thing or the other—probably he meant . . . for he was taking up the red chair. He lifted it high and hung it casually on the handle of a scythe, which, in turn, hung to the beam overhead. An unbroken rung of the chair thereby lay at his eye level. He started the lathe, and with four sure sweeps and five confident pauses, he duplicated the unbroken rung complete to its dowelled ends. He stopped the machine, slapped away collet and tailstock and tried the new rung for size. Freehand, with a keyhole saw, he cut away excess at the tips. It fitted. He took it to the glue pot, dipped the ends, returned and set it in place; then, with simultaneous blows right and left, he drove it home. A war surplus quartermaster's canvas belt plus a suitcase clasp of the over-center type formed a clamp for it. He left it where it hung, and in his strange way—he seemed never to move quickly, but all the same, could loom up over a man in a rush—he rounded on Smith. "You want her back?"

"Oh God," said Jody Smith softly, "I do."

"Hmp." Noat moved to the other end of the counter and gingerly capped the hot glue pot. "You need her," Smith thought he said.

Smith frowned. "Isn't that what I just said?"

"Nope."

Jody Smith's quick petulance evaporated as quickly as it had formed; again he found himself fumbling for whatever it was this creature seemed to mean, or almost meant. "I said I want her back."

"I know. You didn't say you need her."

"It's the same thing."

"No, it ain't."

Half angry, half amused, Smith said, "Oh come on, now. Who'd split hairs about a thing like that?"

"Some people might." He paused, looking at a piece of junk he pulled from a box. "Gorwing, he would."

"Gorwing, he won't," said Smith with some asperity. "Look, I don't want this talked all over with the likes of that Gorwing."

Noat gave a peculiar chuckle. "Gorwing wouldn't talk about it. He'd just *know*."

"I don't get you. He'd just—know? Know what?"

"If you should want something. Or need it."

Smith wagged his head helplessly. "I never know when you're kidding."

"This thing," said Noat soberly, staring at the object in his hand—it seemed to be the ring-shaped, calibrated "card" from a marine compass—"got three hundred and sixty degrees on it. More than any college graduate in the country." Without moving anything but his eyes, he regarded Smith. "Am I kidding?"

In spite of himself, Smith felt moved to laughter. "I don't know." Sobering then, and anxious, "Have you any idea where she might have—"

"I really couldn't say," interjected the proprietor. "Here's Gorwing."

"Oh, for God's sake," Smith muttered.

Gorwing banged in, stopped, stared at Smith. He passed his hand over his eyes and muttered, "Oh, for God's sake."

Then both men turned to Noat, redly regarding his sudden burst of merriment.

"You settin' on a feather?" rasped Gorwing.

"Just listening to the echoes," answered Noat, grinning. Then a quick concern enveloped his features. He leaned forward and watched Gorwing bend his head, gingerly touch the back of his neck. "What is it— him?"

"Him?" Gorwing glanced insultingly at Smith. "Him, too, you might say. You doing anything?"

"What do you want?" asked Noat.

"Let's take a ride."

Noat, too, glanced at Smith, but not with insult. "Sure," he said. "Go on out to the car. Be with you soon's I . . . got something to finish."

Gorwing glanced inimically at Smith again. "Don't waste no time, now," he said, and slung out.

Smith made a relieved and disgusted sighing sound like *zhe-e-e-e!* and shrugged like shuddering. Noat came around the counter and stood close, as if his proximity could add a special urgency to what he had to say. "Mister Smith, you want to see your wife again? You want her to come back?"

"I *told* you—"

"I believe you, especially now. Some other time we'll talk about it all you want. Now if you want to get her back, you go with Gorwing, hear? You drive him where he wants to go."

"*Me?* Not on your life! I want no part of it, and I bet neither does he."

"You just tell him, it's with you or not at all; you tell him I said so."

"Look, I think—"

"Please, Mister Smith, don't think; not now—there isn't time. Just get out there."

"This is the craziest thing I ever heard of."

"You're absolutely right." Noat physically turned Smith around and faced him to the door. Outside, a horn blared. The sound seemed to loop and lock lasso-like round the confused and upset Smith. He allowed it to pull him outside. He might then have been frightened if he had been given a chance to think, but Gorwing roared at him: "Where's G-Note?"

"You come in my car or not at all," Smith parrotted, his voice far more harsh than he had intended. He then marched to his car, got in and started the motor.

Livid, Gorwing sprang out of the other car. "G-Note!" he bawled at the unresponsive store front, then cursed and ran to Smith's car and slammed inside.

"Whose stupid idea was this?" he snarled.

White and shaken, but, feeling that in some way he had already tipped over the lip of some long slide, Smith said, "Not mine. You going some place?"

Gorwing hunched back against the door, as far from Smith as he could get. "You know the Thruway exit southbound?"

"All right."

He turned out into the street and right at the main avenue. Once or twice he glanced at his passenger, the slick black hair, the fevered dark eyes, the lips ever

curled back from the too-sharp, too-white teeth. It was
a tormented, dangerous kind of face, and the posture—
this had been true as he had seen Gorwing stand, walk,
turn, sit—was always one of imminent attack, like some
small furious cornered animal.

He knew a short cut just here, and was on it before
he quite realized he had come so far. He swung the
wheel abruptly and turned into Midland Avenue, and
from the corner of his eye, seemed to see the feral silhouette of his passenger sink and disappear. Astonished, he glanced at Gorwing, to find him bent almost
double, his hands clasping the back of his neck, his eyes
screwed shut.

"You feel sick?" He applied the brakes.

Gorwing unlaced the fingers behind his neck and,
without opening his eyes, freed a hand for some violent semaphore. "Just drive," came his strained, hissing whisper. Puzzled beyond bearing, Smith drove.
Was Gorwing in pain? Or—could this be it—was he
hiding? Who from? There was a football field and a
high school on the left, a row of houses—mostly nurses'
residences for the nearby hospital—on the right. No
one seemed to be paying special attention to the car.

Two blocks further on Gorwing slowly sat up.

"You all right now?"

In a very, very quiet voice, a deathly, a deadly voice,
Gorwing spoke. He tipped the side of his mouth toward Smith as he spoke, but stared straight ahead. He
said, "Don't you ever drive me near the hospital. Not
ever."

Crazy as a coot, thought Smith. "Nobody told me."

"I'm telling you."

They came to the underpass and crossed beneath the
Thruway, and Gorwing came out of himself enough

to lean forward and scan the road and the sides of the road, ahead. Suddenly he pointed. "There he is. Pull over there."

Smith saw a young man in a grimy flannel suit and a white sport shirt, standing on the grassy shoulder just by the Thruway exit. There was a suitcase with a broken clasp on the grass by his feet. Smith pulled off the pavement and stopped.

The man picked up his suitcase and came toward them, trying to smile. "Give us a lift into town?"

Gorwing's tongue darted out to wet his lips, and his eyes seemed to grow even brighter. He waited until the man was abreast of the car, was even elevating his suitcase to let it precede him into the back seat, then sprang out and, chest arched, eyes flaming, blocked the man. "Lift hell," he snarled, "this town wouldn't give a cup o' water to the likes of you. Don't you set foot in it. We don't wancha."

The stranger slitted his eyes. "Now wait, Mac, you wait a minute here. Who the hell you think you are? You own this—"

"Git," said Gorwing, and his voice descended to something like the hissing, strained note that Smith had heard in the car. He mouthed his words—spittle ran suddenly from the corner of his mouth. As he spoke he walked, and as he walked the other man backed away. "You gawd . . . damn . . . junky . . . you think you can come here and pick up a fix, well this place is cold turkey for you and you'd better be on your way out of it, never mind who I am, I killed a man once."

The man tried to shout him down, but Gorwing kept talking, kept crouching forward. "We're stayin' right here to see you walk up the pike or down the pike or hitch a ride, I don't care which way, an' don't think you c'n slide into town without my knowin', I got guys spotted all over town and your life ain't worth a bar o' soap if you so much as show your face let alone tryin' to find a pusher. There ain't no pusher an' if you meet another gawd damn hophead you c'n pass the word—" but it was pointless to go on; suitcase and all, the man had turned by then and fled. Gorwing put his thumbs in his belt and watched the hitchhiker, white-faced, scampering to the northbound lane. Then Gorwing sighed, and turned tiredly back to the car.

"What a blistering," breathed the thunderstruck Smith as Gorwing got in and fell back on the seat. "Who was that?"

"Never saw him before in my life," said Gorwing absently. With great tenderness he touched the back of his neck. He looked at Smith by rolling his fevered eyes, as if the neck were too tender to disturb. "I never killed a man," he said. "I just say that to scare 'em."

A thousand questions pressed on Smith's tongue, but he swallowed all but, "You want to go back now?"

"How's our li'l buddy doing?"

Smith peered down the ramp. Through the underpass, he could see the grimy-white of the hitchhiker's clothes. "He's still—no wait, I think he's got a lift."

Gorwing joined him in peering. They saw a green Dodge slow and stop, and the man climb in. "And good riddance," murmured Gorwing.

"I don't think he'll be back," said Smith, for something to say.

"He'll wish he didn't if he does," said Gorwing, so off-handedly that Smith knew the man, the episode, the whole subject was leaving Gorwing's mind; and in a way this was the most extraordinary part of this inexplicable episode, for Smith knew that he himself would never forget it. Gorwing said, "Drive."

Smith made a slightly illegal turn and got the car headed back toward town. When he saw the yellow and black HOSPITAL ENTRANCE—500 FEET sign, he turned left and went into a long detour. Gorwing sat abstractedly, and Smith was certain he had not noticed the special effort he was making, until they turned back again on to Midland Avenue, well past, and Gorwing said, "Hospitals, they give me the creeps."

"Me, too," said Smith, remembering a tonsillectomy when he was fourteen—his only contact with the healing arts in all his life. Gorwing laughed at him—a singularly unpleasant and mirthless laugh. Anything in Smith that was about to formulate conversation— maybe even a question out of his vast perplexity—dried up. Smith's petulant pink underlip protruded, and he drove without speaking until they pulled up in front of the Anything Shoppe. Smith had never been so glad to see anything in his life. He had had, as of now, exactly all he could take of this man.

He swung his door open but "Oh, hell," Gorwing said. He said it in the tones of a man who has conducted a theater party in from the suburbs and finds, under the marquee, that he has forgotten the tickets. In spite of himself, "What's the matter?" asked Smith.

"Shut up," said Gorwing. Suddenly he closed his eyes and said again, "Oh hell." Then he opened his eyes and snapped, "Get goin'. *Quick.*"

Reflexively Smith shut the door, then demanded of himself *why?* Argumentatively he asked, "Where do you want to go?"

"*Move,* will ya?" He waved vaguely toward Hook Mountain. "Up that way. I'll tell you."

"I don't see—"

Gorwing's words tumbled out so fast they were almost indistinguishable. "Dammit you want somebody should be dead it's your fault you didn't jump when I said jump now *drive!*"

The car was started and heading north before Smith was aware of it, so stunned was he by this hot spurt of language. When a man speaks like that, you want to throw your hands up over your face as if you had seen raging heat through sudden cracks in something you knew, too late, might explode.

A mile later Smith asked timidly, "What do you mean, dead?"

"Your place," Gorwing growled, directing, not responding.

They wheeled into the private road and up the hill. *Dead? My place?* Smith was terrified. "Listen—"

"You got any rope?" Gorwing snapped.

"Rope?" Smith repeated stupidly. He went into his own driveway in a power-slide; he hadn't known he could drive like that. "No, I haven't got any rope. What—"

"Oh, you wouldn't," spat Gorwing. "Chains. You got tire chains?"

"I don't—yes. In the trunk." He braked to a slithering stop in the turnaround. Gorwing was out of the car while it was still sliding, and tugging at the trunk lid. He roared to find it locked. Smith tumbled out with the keys and opened it. Gorwing flung him aside in his dive as he clawed through the trunk, throwing tire iron, jack pedestal, a can of hydraulic fluid behind him like a digging dog. The chains were in a cloth sack; he up-dumped the sack, shook out the chains, hooked the end of one into the end of the other, draped them over his shoulder and sprinted down toward the house.

"Wait, you—" gasped Smith, and trotted after him.

Gorwing passed the house and plunged across the

lower lawn into the woods, Smith after him, already panting. "Hey, watch yourself, that's full of poison ivy back there!"

Gorwing was already out of sight in the rank woods below the house.

Stumbling, gasping, Smith floundered after him, until he came to the edge of the cliff that overlooked the broad Hudson. At this point it was sheer about a hundred feet, then slanted down and away in a mass of weed-grown rubble almost to the railroad tracks. For a moment he thought Gorwing must have plunged straight over the edge, but then he saw him working his way along the ragged brink to the right.

"Hang on! Hang on!" Gorwing yelled. Totally perplexed, Smith looked around him for whatever it was he was supposed to hang on to and failed to find it. He shrugged and stumbled after the man. Gorwing kept bellowing to hang on. Suddenly Smith saw him fall to his knees and crawl to the crumbling lip of the precipice. He yelled again, then moved on a couple of feet and hooked a free end of the tire chains to itself around the trunk of a foolhardy pine tree with a ten-inch bole, which grew bravely at the lip of disaster.

At last, Smith reached Gorwing, who had hunkered down with his back to the tree. He had described the man to himself before as "fevered"—he now looked sick as well; there was a difference. "What are you—"

Gorwing motioned toward the drop. "You'll have to do it. I can't stand high places."

"Do what?"

Gorwing pointed again. Smith heard a weak bleating sound that seemed to come from everywhere. But it was specifically outward that Gorwing had pointed. So he fell to his knees and crawled to the edge and looked over.

Eight or ten feet below him he saw the chalk-white, tear-streaked face of a thirteen- or fourteen-year-old boy. The child was hanging by his hands to a protruding root, which angled so sharply downward that it was clear no grip could last too long on it. The boy's toes were dug into loose earth, a fresh damp scar of which surrounded his feet and, widening, showed where to his left a ledge had fallen away. To his right was rock, almost sheer, and without a handhold.

"Hang on!" yelled Smith, at least half again as loud and urgently as Gorwing had. He caught up the end of the chain and lowered it carefully down. At its fullest extent it reached about to the boy's belt-line. Smith looked at Gorwing, who looked back out of sick black eyes. "You got to," he said in strained tones, "I tell you I can't. I just can't."

Smith, whose usual activities involved nothing more strenuous than stamp tongs, found himself on his stomach, hanging his legs over, hunting wildly with his toes for the rungs formed by the crosslinks of the tire chain. Then he was stepping down, while the earth and grass of the edge rose up and obscured Gorwing like some crazy inverted theater curtain. "Hang on," he said, and was startled when the boy answered, "Okay . . ." because that remark had been for himself.

Tire chains may be roughly the size and shape of a small ladder, but they take unkindly to it. The rungs roll and their parts pinch, and the whole thing swings and bends alarmingly; *you* know they won't break, but do *they*? Too soon the next rung under his seeking foot just—wasn't, and he withdrew the foot from nothing-at-all and stood on the last crosslink, gulping air. He was then of a mind to freeze to his shaky perch and stay there until somebody else figured a way out, but there came a whimper nearby and he saw clods and stones spin sickeningly down and away from the boy's toes. He glanced at the boy's face, saw and would forever see the muddy pallor, the fear-bulged eye, the lips gone whiter than the tanned cheeks. The youngster's foothold was gone, and only his grip on the slanted root held him. Afterward, Smith was to reflect that, if the kid had been standing on anything solid, he would never in life have been able to figure out a way to bring him in; but now he *had* to, so he did.

"Lift your foot!" he screamed. "Give me your foot!" The foot was already dangling, but for an endless, mindless moment the boy stretched downward with it, trying to make a toehold if he could not find one; then Smith screamed again, and the boy brought the foot up slowly, shakily . . . and he said, "My hands, I can't . . ." but then Smith had the foot, leaning far sidewise to get it; he lifted it, thrust it through the last "rung" down to the knee. One more reach, and he had the skinny upper arm in a grip that astonished both of them. "Let go," he panted, and the boy let go; it may well be that he could not have held on any longer to the root if he had wanted to. With the release, the chains swung nauseatingly sidewise; with one hand Smith ground steel into his own flesh, with the other drove flesh into the arm-bone; but he had the boy, now, thrust the arm through the next rung. "Hold with your arms, not your hands," he said through his teeth.

When they stopped swinging, Smith freed his hand from the boy's biceps. It took a concentrated effort, so clamped, so cramped, was his hysterical hand. "Now rest," he said to both, for both of them. The boy kept whimpering, a past-tears meaningless, habitual kind of sound, dry and probably unfelt. Some measureless time later he helped the boy get his other leg into the little twisted square of chain, so that he sat and whimpered, while Smith stood and panted, for however long it took to be able to think again. Then Smith had the boy stand up inside the circle of his arms, and climb until his buttocks were at the level of Smith's chest. Then they climbed together, Smith urging the boy to sit back on him when he had to, half-lifting him when they got the strength and the courage, each interminable time, to try another rung. And when at last the boy tumbled up and over and was, by Gorwing, snatched back from the edge, Smith had to stop achingly and wearily ponder out what had happened to the weight and presence of him, before he could go on.

Gorwing snatched him, too, away from the edge, where he lay laughing weakly.

"You," said Gorwing darkly, "you real gutsy."

"*Me?*"

"I couldn'. Not ever, I could *never* do that." He made a sudden vague gesture, startling in its aimlessness, a jolting contrast to his vulpine appearance and harsh voice. "I never had much guts."

Smith held his peace, as does one in the presence of evidence too great for immediate speculation. He thought of Gorwing standing up to him about the hundred-dollar fare, and of Gorwing ravening, tearing, lashing out at the hitchhiking dope addict. Yet there was no mistaking his sincerity in what he said—nor in this frank compliment to him, Smith—a man who had, up until now, stimulated only open disgust. He promised himself he would think about it later. He said to the boy, "How do you feel, kid?"

"Gee, all right." The boy shuddered. "Ain't going to do *that* again."

"What were you doing?"

"Aw. Bunch of Nyack kids, they bet nobody could climb the cliff. I didn't say nothing, but I thought I could, so I tried it."

Smith stood up, held gingerly to the tree trunk and peered over. "Where are they?"

"Oh gosh, I wouldn't try it when anyone's around. I just wanted to see if I could before I opened my trap about it."

"So no one knew you were there!"

The boy grinned shakily. "You did."

Gorwing and Smith shared a glance; to Smith it meant nothing, but Gorwing rose abruptly and barked, "Let's get out of here." Smith sensed his sudden desire to change the subject, just as he sensed the impact of the boy's refusal to change the subject: "Hey, how *did* you know I was there?"

Gorwing half turned; Smith thought he sensed that glance again, but when he tried to meet it it was gone. "Heard you yellin'," Gorwing said gruffly.

"I live right here," said Smith. It satisfied the boy completely, but for the very first time Smith saw Gorwing look astonished. Yes, and in a way pleased.

They stopped at his house for something cool to drink, and then got in the car to return to Nyack; the boy said he lived on Castle Heights Avenue. There was surprisingly little talk. Neither Gorwing nor Smith seemed to know how to talk to a thirteen-year-old—a rare talent, at best, rare even among thirteen-year-olds —yet what occupied Smith's mind could hardly be discussed in his presence.

Gorwing. This rough, mad, strange, unpredictable Gorwing . . . you couldn't like him; and Smith knew he did not. Yet through him, with him, Smith had shared something new—new, yes, and rich. He had . . . it was as if he had had a friend for a moment there, working so dangerously together . . . and the work was for someone else; that had something to do with it. . . .

Friend. . . . Smith knew many people, and he had no enemies, and so he had thought he had had friends; but for a moment now he got a glimpse of the uncomfortable fact that he had no friends. Never had. Even . . . even Eloise. Husband and wife they were, lovers they had been—hadn't they?—but could he honestly say that he and Eloise had ever been friends?

He sank for a moment into a viscous caldron of scalding loneliness. *Eloise* . . .

"Hey." Gorwing's harsh note crashed into his reverie. "How we get this young feller to keep his mouth shut?"

"Me?" said the boy.

"You better keep your mouth shut, that's all," said Gorwing ominously.

Smith had no experience in talking to boys, but he could see this was the wrong tack. The kid was edging away from Gorwing, and his eyes were too wide. Smith said quickly, "He's right. I don't know your mother, sonny, but I'd say she'd be worried sick if you told her the story. Or maybe just mad."

"Yeah, maybe." He looked warmly at Smith, then timidly at Gorwing. "Yeah, I guess you're right. . . . Can't I tell *nobody*?"

"I'd as soon you didn't."

"Well, anything you say," said the boy. He swallowed and said again, "Anything . . ." and then, "That's my house. The white one."

Smith stopped well away from the house. "Hop out, so no one sees you in the car. So long."

"So long." The boy walked away a slow pace, then turned back. "I don't even know your names."

"Delehanty," said Smith. And Gorwing said solemnly, "Me, too."

"Well," said the boy uneasily, "well, thanks, then," and moved toward the white house.

Smith backed into a nearby driveway and headed back toward the shop.

Gorwing said truculently, "How come you covered for me like that?"

"I had the idea you wanted it that way. Up on the cliff I got that idea."

"Yeah. . . . You know all the time what people want?"

"I don't think," said Smith slowly, with a frankness that stung his eyes, "I ever tried before."

They rolled along for what seemed a long, companionable moment. Then Smith added, "You don't always help people out for money, do you?"

Gorwing shrugged, rolled down his window, and spat. "Only when I can get it. Oh man, could I use some about now."

"This," said Smith bitterly, "is my taxicab this time."

"Oh, I wasn't asking you for nothing. You watch yourself, Smith. I'm no panhandler."

Smith drove self-consciously, carefully. He knew his face was pink, and he hated himself for it. He wondered if he could say anything to this madman without making him angry. Angrier. He asked, without malice, "What would you do with money?"

"Get drunk," said Gorwing, and immediately glanced at Smith's face. "Oh my God," he said disgustedly, "he believes me. I never drink anything. . . . What would I do with money?" he mused. " 'Pends how much. Now there's a couple, the old man is dying.

I mean, he can't last, not much more. The woman, she stays by him ever minute, don't go out even to buy food. Somebody don't go to the store for 'em, throw 'em a couple skins now and then, they . . . oh, you wouldn't know."

No, Smith wouldn't know. He had never been in need . . . or in danger, before today. Turning into Midland Avenue, he glanced down a side street toward the river, where the wide-lawned pleasant houses gave way to the shabby-decent, the tenement, the shack. He had never done that before, not to *see* them. And then, the need you could see, starting with the shacks, was, when you came to think about it, surely not all the need there was; need comes in so many colors and kinds. He brought the thought back up to the crisp-tended, tree-shaded homes on the Avenue and wondered what it was like to live in this world instead of—of whatever it was he had been doing.

He stopped in front of the Anything Shoppe, and they got out. "Here," Smith said. He took out his wallet and found a twenty-dollar bill. He looked at Gorwing and suddenly took out the ten, too—all he had with him.

Gorwing did not thank him. He took the money and said, "Well, all right!" and marched off.

Smith was still wagging his head as he entered the shop.

"I know how you feel," said G-Note, grinning.

"What *is* he?"

G-Note grunted. "I never did really know, myself."

"I never thought I'd say this, but I sort of like him." Smith was feeling very warm inside about all this.

Oddly enough, the remark brought no smile this

time. "I don't know if you can really *like* Gorwing," said Noat thoughtfully. "He sometimes . . . but anyway, tell me what happened."

Smith related his afternoon. Noat nodded sagely. "Junkies," he nodded at one point. "He can't stand 'em. Runs 'em out of town every time."

At the end of his story, Smith told him about the money. "Is that on the level, Mr. Noat? Or will he just go on a toot?"

"No, it's on the level. If he keeps out any for himself, it'll be what he barely needs."

"Doesn't he have a job or something?"

Noat shook his big head. "No job. No home, not what you might call a place of his own. Moves around all the time, furnished rooms, back of the poolhall, here in the shop sometimes. I don't think he ever leaves town, though."

"Mr. Noat, how does he do it?"

Noat cocked his head on one side. "Didn't you ask him?"

Smith laughed weakly. "No." Then, with a sudden surge of candor, "Tell you the truth, I was afraid to."

"Tell you the truth, I'm afraid to, too," said Noat. "He . . . well, between you and me, I think he thinks he's some sort of freak. Or, anyway, he's afraid people will think that. He never lets anybody get close to him. He always does what he can to hide how he does what he does. Usually by blowing up in your face."

"He must . . . he seems to do a lot of good."

"Yes . . ." There was a reservation in the ugly man's voice.

"Well, doggone it, what *is* it he does?"

"He, well, hears when somebody needs something, or maybe you might say smells it. I don't know. I don't know as I care much, except it works. Heck, you don't have to know how everything works—by the time you did, you'd be too old to work it." He turned away, and Smith thought for a moment he had closed the subject, but he said, without turning around, "Only thing I'm sure of, he knows the difference between wanting something and needing it."

"Want . . . you asked me that!"

"I did. I asked Gorwing, too, although maybe you don't remember."

"Eloise . . . you mean he'd know whether I—need her, or just want her? Him?"

Noat chuckled. "Feels like a sort of invasion of privacy, doesn't it? It is and it isn't . . . what he knows, however he knows it, it isn't like anyone else knowing it. That Gorwing . . . but he does a lot of good, you know."

"I don't doubt it."

"Calla Pincus, she thinks he's some sort of saint."

"Who's she?"

"Girl he—well, she was going to kill herself one time, and he stopped her. She'd do anything for him. So would the Blinker—he's kind of a poolhall rat— and there's old Sarge, that's a track walker for the West Side Line . . . I mean, he has sort of a raggle-taggle army, all through the town, that've learned to ask no questions and jump to do what he says. Sometimes for pay. And Doc Tramble, and one of the teachers at the high school and . . . and me, I guess—"

"And me."

Noat laughed. "So welcome to the fold."

"All these years in this town," Smith marveled, "and I never guessed this was going on. Mr. Noat . . . does he know where my wife is?"

"Did you ask him?"

Smith shook his head. "Somehow I . . . I was afraid to ask him that, too."

"You better. You need her—you know that and I do and he does. I think you should ask him. . . . Now can I ask you something?"

"Oh, sure."

"You never went to the police or anything. How come?"

Smith looked down at his hands and closed them, then his eyes. He said in a low voice, "I guess because . . . You know, she said to me, whatever had happened, she still wanted me to be happy. I imagine I wanted the same thing for her. It was something she had to do; I didn't think I should stop her."

"But you're looking now."

"Not with police."

"Hey, he's coming. Ask him. Go ahead—ask him."

Smith turned eagerly to the door as Gorwing banged in. "Hi!" He felt warm, friendly—pleasurably scared—anticipatory. Gorwing utterly ignored him.

Noat frowned briefly and said, "Hey boy. Smitty there, he's got something to ask you."

"He has?" Gorwing did not even look around.

Smith hesitated, then caught Noat's encouraging nod. Timidly, he asked, "Mr. Gorwing . . . do you know where my wife is?"

Gorwing flicked him with a black glance and showed his white teeth. "Sure." Then he turned his full cruel smile on Smith and said, "She don't need you."

Smith blinked as if something had flashed before his eyes. His mouth was dry inside, and outside shivery. He wanted to say something but could not.

Noat growled, "That ain't what he asked you, Gorwing. He says do you know where she is."

"Oh sure," said Gorwing easily, and grinned again. "She got a cold-water walk-up over on High Avenue, 'long with the guy she's livin' with."

Smith had never in his life physically attacked anyone, but now he grunted, just as if he had been kicked in the stomach, and rushed Gorwing. He struck out, a wild, round, unpracticed blow, but loaded with hysteria and hate. It never reached Gorwing, but planted itself instead in the region of Noat's left shoulder blade, for Noat, moving with unbelievable speed for so large a man, had vaulted the counter and come between them. He came, obviously, not to protect anyone, but to launch his own attack. "You lousy little rat, you didn't have to do that. Now you get out of here," he rumbled, as with one hand he opened the door and with the other literally threw Gorwing outside. Gorwing tried to keep his balance but could not; he fell heavily, rolled, got up. His face was so white his black hair looked almost blue; still he grinned. Then he was gone.

Noat closed the door and came to Smith. "So now you know."

"El—Eloise is . . ." and he began to cough.

"Oh, not that! I mean, now you know about Gorwing. How can you figure it? All he does is take care of what people need . . . and there's no kindness in him."

"Eloise is—"

"Your wife is taking care of an old sick man who'll be dead any time now."

"Who," Smith cried, agonized. "*What* old man?"

"That you just gave the money for."

"I've got to find her," whispered Smith, and then heard what Noat had said. "You mean—*that* old man? Wh—why, he told me it was an old *couple!*"

"I bet he didn't."

"You! *You* know where she is! You knew all the time."

Noat spread his hands unhappily. "You never asked me."

Smith's scorn made him appear a sudden four inches taller. "Quit playing games!"

"Okay . . . okay." The big man looked completely miserable. "I just didn't want to hurt you, that's all." At Smith's sharp look, he said "Honest. Honest. . . . Gorwing, he's right, you know. She doesn't need you. I wish you didn't make me tell you that. I'm sorry." He went back behind the counter, as if he could comfort himself with the tools, the clutter back there.

"You better tell me the whole thing," whispered Smith.

"Well . . . she, Mrs. Smith I mean, she came to me that day. She was all . . . mixed up. I don't think she meant to spill anything, but she sort of . . . couldn't hold it." He put up a swift hand when Smith would have interrupted. "Wait, I'm telling this all wrong. What I'm trying to say, she came here because she just didn't know where else to go to. She said something about 'Anything Shoppe'; she wanted to know if 'anything' meant . . . *anything*. She said she had to have a job, something to do. She said never mind the money, just enough to scrape along, but something to *do;* that's what she needed."

"What she needed."

"I know what you're thinking. Yeah, Gorwing knew she needed something, and just what it was, too . . . y'see," he said earnestly, "he's always right. Even the lousy things he does sometimes, they're always right.

Or at least . . . there's always a reason." He stopped, as if to ponder it out for himself.

"Look," said Smith, suddenly, painfully kneading his cheeks, "whatever it is you have to tell me, tell me. I'm all mixed up . . . and . . . and *where is she?*" Then he opened his blue eyes very wide—oddly like those of the boy he had saved on the cliff when Gorwing had frightened him—and said piteously, "You mean she really doesn't need me? Gorwing was right?"

G-Note crouched over, elbows on the counter, his big hands holding each other in front of him.

He said, "What she needed, what she needed more than anything in the world, she needed something to take care of. You—well, she tried to take care of you, but— Don't you see what I mean?"

There was silence for a long time. Smith felt that somehow, if he could pull together the churned-up pieces of his mind, he might be able to turn it to this, make some sense out of it. He tried very hard, and at last was able to say, "You mean, when you come right down to it, there . . . was never very much for her to do for me."

"Oh, you got it. You got it. You . . . well, she told me some things. She cried, I guess she didn't mean to say anything, but I guess—she just had to. She said you could cook better'n she could."

"*What?*"

"Well, things you liked to eat, you could. And those were all the things you ever wanted. She took care of the house, but you'd 'a done just the same things if she wasn't there. She never felt she really *had* to . . ."

"But this old man—who's *he?*"

"One of Gorwing's . . . you know. Gorwing found

him down by the tracks. Sick, wore out. Needing somebody to take care of him—*needing* it, you see? Not for long . . . Doc Tramble, he says he don't know how the old fellow hung on this long."

"God," said Smith, stinging with chagrin, "is that what she needed? Maybe I should be dying—she'd be happy with me then."

"Ah, knock that off. She's only like most people, she has to make a difference to somebody. She makes a difference to that old man, and she knows it."

"She made a difference to me," whispered Smith, and then something lit up inside him. He stared at Noat. "But she never knew it." Suddenly he leaped to his feet, walked up, walked back, sat again bolt upright, holding himself as if he were full of coiled springs. "What's the matter with me? You know what I did, I said she had somebody with her while I was at the Elks' that night, you know, the night you picked me up in the car. That's why she left." He hit himself on the forehead with sharp knuckles. "I know she didn't have anyone, she wouldn't! So what made me think of it? Why all of a sudden did I have to think of it, and even when I knew I was wrong, why did I have to go for her, curse at her, call her names the way I did, till she had to leave . . . why?" he shouted.

"You really want me to tell you?" Then Noat looked away from Smith's frantic, twisted face and shook his head. "I don't *know*," he said carefully, "I only know what I think. I don't know everything . . . I don't know you very much. All right?"

"Yes, I understand that. Go ahead."

"Well, then." Noat watched his big brown hands press and slide on the counter until they squeaked, as if they had ideas under them and could express the

words by squeezing. He raised them and looked under
them and folded them and looked at Smith. "You hear
a lot of glop," he said carefully, "about infantile
this and adult that, and acting like a grownup. I've
thought a lot about that. Like how you've got to be
adult about this or that arrangement with people or
the world or your work or something. Like they'd say
you never had an adult relationship with the missus.
Don't get mad! I don't mean—well, hell, how adult is
two rabbits? I don't mean the sex thing." He opened
his hands to look for more words, and folded them
again. "Most people got the wrong idea about this
'adult' business, this 'grownup' thing they talk about
but don't think about. What I'm trying to say, if a
thing is alive, it changes all the time. Every single
second it changes; it grows or rots or gets bigger or
grows hair in its armpits or puts out buds or sheds
its skin or something, but when a thing is living, it
changes." He looked at Smith, and Smith nodded. He
went on:

"What I think about you, I think somewhere along
the line you forgot about that, that you had to go on
changing. Like when you're little, you keep getting
bigger all the time, you get promoted in school; you
change; good. But then you get out, you find your
spot, you got your house, your wife, your kind of
work, then there's nothing around you any more says
you have to change. No class to get promoted to. No
pants grown too small. You think you can stop now,
not change any more." Noat shook his craggy head.
"Nothing alive will stand for that, Smitty."

"Well, but why did I think she . . . why did I say
that about—some man with her, all that?"

Noat shrugged. "I don't know all about you," he

said again. "Just sort of guessing, but suppose you'd stopped, you know, *living.* Something's going to kick up about that. It don't have to make a lot of sense; just kick up. Get mad about something. Your wife with some man—now, that's not nice, that's not even true, but it's a *living* kind of thing, you see what I mean? I mean, things change around the house then —but good; altogether; right *now.*"

"My God," Smith breathed.

" 'Course," said Noat, "sooner or later you have to get over it, face things as they really are. Or as they really ain't." He thought again for a time, then said, "Take a tree, starts from a seed, gets to be a stalk, a sapling, on up till it's a hundred feet tall and nine feet through the trunk; it's still growing and changing until one fine day it gets its growth; it's grown up: it's —dead. So the whole thing I'm saying is, this adult relationship stuff they talk about, it's not that at all. It's *growing* up that matters, not *grown*up. . . . Man can get along alone for quite a long time 'grownup'— taking care of himself. But if he takes in anyone else, he's . . . well, he's got to have a piece missing that the other person supplies all the time. He's got to need that, and he's got to have something that's missing in the other person that they need. So then the two of them, they're one thing now . . . and still it's got to be like a living thing, it's got to change and grow and be alive. Nothing alive will stand for being stopped. So . . . excuse me for butting in, but you thought you could stop it and it blew up on you."

Smith stared silently at the big man, then nodded. "I see. But now what?"

"You want to know where she is?"

"Sure. By the Lord, now I can. . . ."

"What's the matter?"

Smith looked at him, stricken. "Gorwing said . . . she didn't need me."

"Gorwing!" snarled Noat. Then he scratched his head. "I see what he meant. She never could take care of you much, and she awful much needs to take care of somebody. Now she's got the old feller. He needs her, God knows. For a little while yet. . . . Gorwing . . . hey! Why d'ye suppose he tried to make you think—you know—about your wife?"

"You know him better than I do."

"It comes to me," said Noat, inwardly amazed. "I see it. I see it. He makes it his business to take care of what people really need, need real bad. Right? Good. How do you do that?"

"Get 'em what they need, I guess."

"That's one way. Two—" he held up fingers—"you get 'em out of range. Like he does with dope addicts. Right? Then—three. You fix it so they just don't feel they need it any more. I mean, if he was to fix it that you got so mad at your wife you wouldn't want ever to see her again—see?"

"That poor little man! He couldn't do that."

"He just tried. He has a gift, Smitty, but that don't mean he's bright."

"It doesn't?" said Smith in tones of revelation. "It's bright enough. I need her—that's one big need, correct? Now, suppose I go find her, take her away from that poor old man. He starts needing her—and she starts needing to take care of somebody again. So—two big needs. That Gorwing, he knows what he's doing. I—I can't do that, Mr. Noat."

"You mean, to the old man?"

"Well, yes, that. But her . . . my wife. I need her. You know that, and I do."

"And Gorwing does."

"Yeah, but she doesn't. God, what do I have to do?
Do I really have to be dying?"

"Living," said George Noat.

You're a freak.

Sometimes for days at a time he could content himself with the thought that all the rest of them were
freaks. Or that, after all, what does anyone do? When
it gets cold, they try to get warm. When they get hungry, they go find something to eat. What people feel,
whatever's crowding them, they get out from under
the best way they can, right? They duck it or move it
or blast it out of the way, or use it on something else
that might be bothering them, right? And what
bothers people is different, one from the other. Hunger
can get to them all and cold and things like that; but
look, one wants some music, some special kind of
music, more than anything else in life, more than a
woman or a drink, while another needs heroin and
another to have a roomful of people clapping their
hands at him. Or needing, needing like life-and-death,
some stupid little thing that would mean nothing to
anyone else—something as little as a couple of words,
like that Calla girl, about to jump off the Tappan Zee
Bridge for wanting somebody to come up to her and
say, "Hey, I need you to do something nobody else
can do." Or needing to feel safe from some something
that lurks inside them, like the Blinker: you'd never
guess it to watch him cuss and laugh and make the
pass, and chalk the cue, just like anybody, but he was
epileptic and he never knew when it was going to hit
him. Or needing defense against things lurking outside of them, like Miss Guelph at the high school,
crazy afraid of feathers, terrified one might touch her.
So the things people need and the things they need to

be safe from, they're all kinds of things: it doesn't make one of them a freak if his special need is a little different.

What if you never heard of anyone with a need just like yours? Does that automatically make you a freak? . . . There are lots of people who have to make it alone, who can't share what they have with anyone. Who can't drive a car for fear that faint-making, aching cloud will suck them down into it when they don't expect it.

Sometimes, too, you can get to believe that the very thing that's wrong with you makes you special. Well, it does, too. You have power over people. Now just how many people in this—or any—town could tell you a little kid two blocks away was lost, and a woman three blocks the other way was looking for him? Or look at the way you found that boy on the cliff—now that boy would be dead right now.

So if you're so special how come old Noat throws you out on your ear?

You're a freak.

Now cut it out. You got it made. You got a nice spot. The town's just big enough so nobody much notices you, just small enough so when that faintness comes, and that ache, and then the picture in your head—of a traffic light or a building front or a green fence or a cliffside—you know just where to go to find the person who has that big noisy need for something. Remember that trip down to Fort Lee? So big, so noisy; God, you almost went out of your head. Plank you down in the middle of New York, say, you'd be dead in a second, all that racket. And the things they need, you'd never know where to get them in a big place, but here, heck, you know where to find anything if it's in town. Or old Noat will get it for you.

What he want to throw you out like that for? Just
trying to shut off the shrieking lonesomeness of that
squirt Smith; him and his Eloise, it gave him a head-
ache.

Ow. Here comes one now. Shut your eyes. Ow, my
neck. Shut your eyes tight, now. See . . . see a . . . see
a street, store-front, green eaves over the window. Felt
carpet slippers, a man's belt. That would be Harry
Schein's Haberdashery on Washington Street. Somebody standing there, needs—what? Sleep, wants to
sleep, for God's sake, gets wide awake soon as hits the
sack . . . a man. Screaming for sleep, frantic for sleep.
Get some sleeping pills, everything closed now. Hey,
this could be worth a buck. Go call Doc Tramble.
Here, phone in the gas station. NY 7 . . . 0 . . . 0 . . .
5 . . . 1.

"Doc? Gorwing here. Got some sleeping pills in
your bag? Oh, nothing serious . . . yes, I know what's
dangerous and what ain't. No, not for me. Oh, five, I
guess. I'll send the Blinker or somebody around for
'em, okay?"

Ow. Guy walking toward Broad street now. Oh boy
does he want some sleep. Where's dime . . . here. Call
poolroom. . . . 4 . . . . 7 . . . . "Hi—Danny? Gorwing. Hey, the Blinker there? Hell. . . . Who else is
around? No . . . Nuh, not her. Smith? What Smith—
you mean that guy's been hanging around G-Note's?
Yeah, put him on.

"Hello—Smitty? Thought you'd be mad. You
wouldn't want to do a little job . . . you would? Well
you'll have to scramble. Get over to Doc Tramble's
and say you want the pills for me. Yeah. Then take
'em over to Fordson Alley and North Broad—you
know, right by the movie—there's a guy there frantic
for 'em. See if you can get a dollar apiece. Sleeping

tablets. Yeah. Hurry now. . . . He's moving, he's
ambling up past the movie. *I* don't know what he
looks like. Just look for a guy looks like he needs
some sleep. Hurry now. See ya."

Now that's a surprise. I thought I'd butched it up
with that Smith but for good. A good boy. Calmed
down, too. Wonder if he's going to pull that wife of
his away from the old man. Hope not. Set up a hell of
a rattle, the two of 'em at once.

So Gorwing ambled through the evening, through
the town. He walked in a cloud of, or in a murmur
of, or under the pressure of, or through the resistance
of the not-mist, not-sound, not-weight, not-fluid
presence of human need. *Want* was there, too, but
want of that kind—two teen-agers yearning for a
front-drive imported car in a show window, a drowsy
child remembering a huge bride-doll in Woolworth's,
the susurrus of desire that whispered up in the wake
of a white-clad blonde who, with her boy-friend, walked
through the lights of the theater marquee—this kind
of want was simply there to be noticed if he cared
to notice it. But the need . . . he watched for it fear-
fully, yet eagerly—for sometimes it paid off. He hoped
that for a while nobody would get hit by a car without getting killed outright, or that some hophead
wouldn't suddenly appear with that rasping, edgy
scream of demand. Ow. Wish Smitty would get to
that guy with the sleeping pills.

Need was a noise to Gorwing. No, not really a
noise. Need was an acid cloud, a swirling blindness.
Need might mount up out of the nighttime village
and make him faint. Need might pay off. Need, other
people's need, hurt Gorwing . . . but then each person
had one or another difference, one or another talent;

this one had perfect pitch and that one had diabetes, and he wasn't, after all, so different from other people.

You're a freak.

Strangely, it was not too easy to be funereal at this funeral. The flowers were sad, of course, such a scrappy little bunch, and the man was saying all the right things . . . and it was sad how easily the men handled the coffin; poor little old man, so wasted away. But you couldn't feel badly about him now; he'd been glad to go, and it was good that he'd had, for those last weeks, just what he'd yearned for for so many sick lonesome years—someone who sat near and brought him things and listened to him ramble on about all the old places and the friends and family who were passed on, dead and gone and yet waiting eagerly for him, some place. No, it wasn't any tragedy. Sweetly sad, that was it . . . oh, such a beautiful day!

Eloise Smith hadn't been out in the fresh air, the sunshine, since . . . *"Eeek!"*

It was a small scream, or rather squeak, and really no one noticed. But Jody, oh Jody was standing right next to her in a dark suit, with his hat—the one they called his Other hat—held over his heart, his head bowed. He looked . . . peaceful.

She bowed her head, too, and they stood quite close together until the man finished saying the old simple words, and the handful of earth went *tsk!*—a polite expression of sympathy—on the coffin lid. Then it was over. *"'Bye, you old dear,"* she said silently but with her heart full.

Then there was Jody. "Oh, Jody. I don't think I—"

"Shh. Eloise, come home. I need you."

"Jody, you're going to make me sound mean, and I don't want to be mean. But you don't need me or anybody, Jody."

Smith moistened his lips, but loosened no special, just-right winning words; he said, could say, only: "I need you. Come home."

"Wait—there's Mr. Gorwing. . . . Wait, Jody; I have to speak to him. Will you wait over there, Jody? Please?"

"Let me stay with you."

"Honey," she said, the wifely word slipping out before she realized it, "he's sometimes sort of . . . funny. Unpredictable. I wish you'd wait over there and let me talk to—"

"He won't mind. We're old friends."

"You know Mr. Gorwing?"

"Sure."

"Oh dear. I didn't know. He . . . he's a kind of saint, you know." When Smith, coolly regarding Gorwing, who was talking to the funeral director, did not answer, she went on nervously—she had to talk, *had* to, oh *why* had he turned up like this, all unexpectedly?—"If anyone's in need at all, he has a way of finding it out; he—"

"I'm in need," said Smith. "I need *you*."

"Jody, *don't*."

"I do," he said softly, earnestly. "You've got to come back. I can't manage without you."

"Oh, that's silly! You have your—"

"I have my nothing, Ellie. I—I gave the money away, almost all of it. I got a job, but I'm only beginning, and the pay isn't much. I'm running a wood lathe in the cabinetmaker's."

"You—*what?*"

"You've got to help; maybe you'll even have to go to work. Would you, if there's no other way? I can't make it without you, Ellie."

What she was going to say through those soft trembling lips he would not know, for Gorwing interrupted. "Miz Smith—you know who he is?"

She flashed a look at her husband and really blushed. Gorwing laughed that wolf's laugh, that barking expression of mirth and hurt, and said, "I'll tell you who he is. He's the only person in the whole world who ever came up to me and asked *me* what *I* needed." He clapped Smith on the shoulder, waved a casual hand at Eloise and walked away toward the cemetery gate. She called him once; he waved his hand but did not turn his face toward them.

"We'll see him again," said Smith. "Ellie . . . will you just let me tell you what this is all about?"

"What *is* it all about?"

"Can I tell you all of it?"

"Oh, very well . . ."

"It'll take about twenty-three years. Oh Eloise—come home."

"Oh, Jody . . ."

The shy man crouched in the hospital stairwell and peered through the crack of the barely-opened door. There were no white-coated figures in the corridor that he could see. He had long ago abandoned the front way, the elevator and all. Slipping in through the fire doors during visiting hours was *much* better. He pushed the door open far enough to let him into the corridor, and let it swing silently closed.

He gasped.

"Hello, Johnny."

Right behind the door as he opened it, oh God, the

doctor. Johnny bit his tongue and stared up into Doc Tramble's face. It blurred.

"Hey now, hold on," said the doctor. "You better come in here and sit down." He took Johnny's forearm—and for a split second they were both acutely aware of Johnny's tearing temptation to snatch it away and run; and of its crushed quelling—and led him across the corridor into an empty private room, where he lowered the sweating visitor into an easy chair. Dr. Tramble pulled up a straight chair and sat close enough to force Johnny's gaze up and into his own.

'I don't know if you can take this, Johnny, all at once, but you're going to have to try."

"I got a second job, nights," said Johnny hollowly. "With that I can catch up some on the bills. Don't put my wife on the charity list, doctor. She couldn't stand it. She—"

"Now you just listen to me, young fella." He reached into the wall, got a paper cup from a dispenser and filled it from the ice-water jet. With his other hand he reached into his side pocket and took out a folded paper, which he planked down on Johnny's knee. "The bill. I want you to look at it."

Painfully, Johnny unfolded it and looked. His jaw dropped. "So much . . ." Then his eyes picked up an additional detail on the paper. "P-p-paid?" he whispered.

"In full," said Dr. Tramble. "That's point one. Point two, Madge gets her operation. MacKinney from the Medical Center got interested in the case. He's going to do it next week. Point three—"

"Her operation . . ."

"Point three," laughed the doctor, "she gets that room to herself now, all paid up, and you have the privilege of telling that to her snide roommate. Point four, here is a check made out to you for five hundred. Drink this," and he pushed the water at him.

Johnny sipped, and over the cup said, "B-but wh-where . . ."

"Let's keep it simple and say it's a special fund for interesting cases from the Medical Center, and you know these endowed institutes—all this money is interest and there's nobody to thank so shut up and get out of here. No—not to see Madge! Not yet. You go down to the office and they'll cash that check for you. Then you grab a taxi and voom down the street and buy flowers and a radio and a big box of dusting powder and a fancy bed jacket. Git!"

Numbly, Johnny walked to the door. Once there, he turned to the doctor, opened his mouth, shook his head, closed his mouth and without a word went for the elevators.

Laughing, the doctor went down the corridor to the telephone booth, dropped a coin, dialed the poolroom.

"Gorwing there?"

"Speaking."

"Tramble. All set."

"Yeah, doc, I know. I know. Oh God, doc, it's so *quiet* in this town . . ."

ABREACTION

I sat at the controls of the big D-8 bulldozer, and I tried to remember. The airfield shoulder, built on a saltflat, stretched around me. Off to the west was a clump of buildings—the gas station and grease rack. Near it was the skeletal silhouette of a temporary weather observation post with its spinning velocimeter and vane and windsock. Everything seemed normal, but there was something *else*. . . .

I could remember people, beautiful people in shining, floating garments. I remembered them as if I had seen them just a minute ago, and yet at a distance; but the memories were of faces close—close. One face —a golden girl; eyes and skin and hair three different shades of gold.

I shook my head so violently that it hurt. I was a bulldozer operator. I was—what was I supposed to be doing? I looked around me, saw the gravel spread behind me, the bare earth ahead; knew, then, that I was spreading gravel with the machine. But I seemed to—to— Look, without the physical fact of the half-done job around me, I wouldn't have known why I was there at all!

I knew where I had seen that girl, those people. I thought I knew . . . but the thought was just where I couldn't reach it. My mind put out searching tendrils for that knowledge of place, that was so certainly there, and the knowledge receded so that the tendrils stretched out thin and cracked with the effort, and my head ached from it.

A big trailer-type bottom-dump truck came hurtling and howling over the shoulder toward me, the huge fenderless driving wheels throwing clots of mud high in the air. The driver was a Puerto Rican, a hefty middle-aged fellow. I knew him well. Well—didn't I? He threw out one arm, palm up, signaling "Where do you want it?" I pointed vaguely to the right, to the advancing edge of the spread gravel. He spun his steering wheel with one hand, put the other on the trip-lever on his steering column, keeping his eyes on my face. As he struck the edge of the gravel fill with his wheels I dropped my hand; he punched the lever and the bottom of the trailer opened up, streaming gravel out in a windrow thirty feet long and a foot deep—twelve cubic yards of it, delivered at full speed. The driver waved and headed off, the straight-gut exhaust of his high-speed Diesel snorting and snarling as the rough ground bounced the man's foot on the accelerator.

I waved back at the Puerto Rican—what was his name? I knew him, didn't I? He knew me, the way he waved as he left. His name—was it Paco? Cruz? Eulalio? Damn it, no, and I knew it as well as I knew my own—

But I didn't know my own name!

Oh hell, oh hell, I'm crazy. I'm scared. I'm scared crazy. What had happened to my head? . . . Everything whirled around me and without effort I remembered about the people in the shining clothes and as my mind closed on it, it evaporated again and there was nothing there.

* * *

Once when I was a kid in school I fell off the
parallel bars and knocked myself out, and when I
came to it was like this. I could see everything and
feel and smell and taste anything, but I couldn't
remember anything. Not for a minute. I would ask
what had happened, and they would tell me, and five
minutes later I'd ask again. They asked me my address so they could take me home, and I couldn't
remember it. They got the address from the school
files and took me home, and my feet found the way
in and up four flights of stairs to our apartment—I
didn't remember which way to go but my feet did. I
went in and tried to tell my mother what was the
matter with me and I couldn't remember, and she
put me to bed and I woke four hours later perfectly
all right again.

In a minute, there on the bulldozer, I didn't get
over being scared but I began to get used to it, so I
could think a little. I tried to remember everything
at first, but that was too hard, so I tried to find
something I could remember. I sat there and let my
mind go quite blank. Right away there was something about a bottom-dump truck and some gravel.
It was there, clear enough, but I didn't know where it
fit nor how far back. I looked around me and there
was the windrow of gravel waiting to be spread. Then
that was what the truck was for; and—had it just
been there, or had I been sitting there for long, for
ever so long, waiting to remember that I must spread
it?

Then I saw that I could remember ideas, but not
events. Events were there, yes, but not in order. No
continuity. A year ago—a second ago—same thing.
Nothing clear, nothing very real, all mixed up. Ideas

were there whatever, and continuity didn't matter. That I could remember an idea, that I could know that a windrow of gravel meant that gravel must be spread; *that* was an idea, a condition of things which I could recognize. The truck's coming and going and dumping, that was an event. I knew it had happened because the gravel was there, but I didn't know when, or if anything had happened in between.

I looked at the controls and frowned. Could I remember what to do with them? This lever and that pedal—what did they mean to me? Nothing, and nothing again . . .

I mustn't think about that. I don't have to think about that. I must think about *what* I must do and not how I must do it. I've got to spread the stone. Here there is spread stone and there there is none, and at the edge of the spread stone is the windrow of gravel. So watching it, seeing how it lay, I let my hands and feet remember about the levers and pedals. They throttled up, raised the blade off the ground, shifted into third gear, swung the three-ton mold-board and its twelve-foot cutting edge into the windrow. The blade loaded and gravel ran off the ends in two even rolls, and my right hand flicked to and away from me on the blade control, knowing how to raise it enough to let the gravel run out evenly underneath the cutting edge, not too high so that it would make a bobble in the fill for the tracks to teeter on when they reached it—for a bulldozer builds the road it walks on, and if the road is rough the machine see-saws forward and the blade cuts and fills to make waves which, when the tracks reach them, makes the machine see-saw and cut waves, which, when the tracks reach them . . . anyway, my hands knew what to do, and my feet; and they did it all the time when I could

only see what was to be done, and could not understand the events of doing it.

This won't do it, I thought desperately. I'm all right,
I guess, because I can do my work. It's all laid out in
front of me and I know what has to be done and my
hands and feet know how to do it; but suppose somebody comes and speaks to me or tells me to go somewhere else, I who can't even remember my own name.
My hands and my feet have more sense than my head.

So I thought that I had to inventory everything I
could trust, everything I knew positively. What were
the things I knew?

The machine was there and true, and the gravel, and
the bottom-dump that brought it. My being there was
a real thing. You have to start everything with the be-
lief that you yourself exist.

The job, the work, they were true things.

Where was I?

I must be where I should be, where I belonged, for
the bottom-dump driver knew me, knew I was there,
knew I was waiting for stone to spread. The airfield
was there, and the fact that it was unfinished. "Airfield" was like a corollary to me, with the runway and
the windsock its supporting axioms, and I had no need
to think further. The people in the shining garments,
and the girl—

But there was nothing about them here. Nothing at
all.

To spread stone was a thing I had to do. But was
that all? It wasn't just spreading stone. I had to spread
it to—to—

Not to help finish the airfield. It wasn't that. It
was something else, something—

Oh. Oh! I had to spread stone to *get* somewhere.

I didn't want to get anywhere, except maybe to a place where I could think again, where I could know what was happening to me, where I could reach out with my mind and grasp those important things, like my name, and the name of the bottom-dump driver, Paco, or Cruz, or Eulalio or maybe even Emanualo von Hachmann de la Vega, or whatever. But being able to think straight again and know all these important things was arriving at a *state* of consciousness, not at a *place*. I knew, I knew, somehow I knew truly, that to arrive at that state I had to arrive at a point.

Suddenly, overwhelmingly, I had a flash of knowledge about the point—not what it was, but how it was, and I screamed and hurt my throat and fell blindly back in the seat of the tractor trying to push away *how* it was.

My abdomen kneaded itself with the horror of it. I put my hands on my face and my hands and face were wet with sweat and tears. Afraid? Have you ever been afraid to die, seeing Death looking right at you; closer than that; have you seen Death turn away from you because He knows you must follow Him? Have you seen that, and been afraid?

Well, this was worse. For this I'd hug Death to me, for He alone could spare me what would happen to me when I reached the place I was going to.

So I wouldn't spread stone.

I wouldn't do anything that would bring me closer to reaching the place where that thing would happen to me. *Had happened* to me. . . . I wouldn't do it. That was an important thing.

There was one other important thing. I must not go on like this, not knowing my name, and what the name of the bottom-dump driver was, and where this airfield and this base were, and all those things.

These two things were the most important things in the world. In *this* world. . . . THIS world. . . .

This world, this world—*other* world. . . .

There was a desert all around me.

Ha! So the airfield wasn't real, and the bottom-dump wasn't real, and the animometer and the grease racks weren't real. Ha! (why worry about the driver's name if he wasn't real?)

The bulldozer was real, though. I was sitting on it. The six big cylinders were ticking over, and the master-clutch lever was twitching rhythmically as if its lower end were buried in something that breathed. Otherwise—just desert, and some hills over there, and a sun which was too orange.

Think, now, think. This desert means something important. I wasn't surprised at being in the desert. That was important. This place in the desert was near something, near an awful something that would hurt me.

I looked all around me. I couldn't see it, but it was there, the something that would hurt so. I wouldn't go through that again—

Again.

Again—that was an important thing. I wouldn't spread stone and reach that place. I wouldn't go through that which had happened to me even if I stayed crazy like I was for the rest of eternity. Let them put me away and tie me up and shake their heads over me and walk away and leave me, and put bars on the windows to slice the light of the crooked moon into black and silver bars on the floor of my cell. I didn't care about all that. I could face the ache of wanting to know about my name and the name of the driver of the bottom-dump (he was a Puerto Rican so his name must be Villamil or Roberto, not Bucyrus-Erie or

Caterpillar Thirteen Thousand) and the people in the shining clothes; I *was* facing all that, and I know how it hurt, but I would not go through that place again and be hurt so much more. Not again. Not again.

Again. Again again again. What is the again-ness of everything? Everything I am doing I am doing again. I could remember that feeling from before—years ago it used to happen to me every once in a while. You've never been to a certain village before, we'll say, and you come up over the crown of the hill on your bicycle and see the way the church is and the houses, and the turn of that crooked cobblestoned street, the shape and tone of the very flowerstems. You know that if you were asked, you could say how many pickets were in the white gate in the blue-and-white fence in the little house third from the corner. All the scientists nod and smile and say you did see it for the second time—a twentieth of a second after the first glimpse; and that the impact of familiarity was built up in the next twentieth of a second. And you nod and smile too and say well, whaddaye know. But you know, you *know* you've seen that place before, no matter what they say.

That's the way I knew it, sitting there on my machine in the desert and not surprised, and having that feeling of again-ness; because I was remembering the last time the bottom-dump came to me there on the airfield shoulder, trailing a plume of blue smoke from the exhaust stack, bouncing and barking as it hurtled toward me. It meant nothing at first, remembering, that it came, nor that it was the same driver, the Puerto Rican; and of course he was carrying the same sized load of the same material. All trips of the bottom-dump were pretty much the same. But there was one thing I remembered—*now* I remembered—

* * *

There was a grade-stake driven into the fill, to guide the depth of the gravel, and *it was no nearer to me than it had ever been.* So that hadn't been the same bottom-dump, back another time. It was the *same time,* all over again! The last time was wiped out. I was on a kind of escalator and it carried me up until I reached the place where I realized about what I had to go through, and screamed. And then I was snatched back and put on the bottom again, at the place where the Puerto Rican driver Señor What's-his-name dumped the gravel and went away again.

And this desert, now. This desert was a sort of landing at the side of the escalator, where I might fall sometimes instead of going all the way to the bottom where the truck came. I had been here before, and I was here again. I had been at the unfinished air base again and again. And there was the other place, with the shining people, and the girl with all those kinds of gold. That was the same place with the crooked moon.

I covered my eyes with my hands and tried to think. The clacking Diesel annoyed me, suddenly, and I got up and reached under the hood and pulled the compression release. Gases chattered out of the ports, and a bubble of silence formed around me, swelling, the last little sounds scampering away from me in all directions, leaving me quiet.

There was a soft thump in the sand beside the machine. It was one of the shining people, the old one, whose forehead was so broad and whose hair was fine, fine like a cobweb. I knew him. I knew his name, too, though I couldn't think of it at the moment.

He dismounted from his flying-chair and came to me.

"Hello," I said. I took my shirt from the seat beside me and hung it on my shoulder. "Come on up."

He smiled and put up his hand. I took it and helped him climb up over the cat. His hands were very strong. He stepped over me and sat down.

"How do you feel?" Sometimes he spoke aloud, and sometimes he didn't, but I always understood him.

"I feel—mixed up."

"Yes, of course," he said kindly. "Go on. Ask me about it."

I looked at him. "Do I—*always* ask you about it?"

"Every time."

"Oh." I looked all around, at the desert, at the hills, at the dozer, at the sun which was too orange. "Where am I?"

"On Earth," he said; only the word he used for Earth meant Earth only to him. It meant *his* Earth.

"I know that," I said. "I mean, where am I really? Am I on that air base, or am I here?"

"Oh, you are here," he said.

Somehow I was vastly relieved to hear it. "Maybe you'd better tell me all about it again."

"You said 'again'," he said, and put his hand on my arm. "You're beginning to realize. . . . Good, lad. Good. All right. I'll tell you once more.

"You came here a long time ago. You followed a road with your big noisy machine, and came roaring down out of the desert to the city. The people had never seen a noisy machine before, and they clustered around the gate to see you come. They stood aside to let you pass, and wondered, and you swung the machine and crushed six of them against the gateposts."

"I *did?*" I cried. Then I said, "I did. Oh, I did."

He smiled at me again. "Shh. Don't. It was a long time ago. Shall I go on?

"We couldn't stop you. We have no weapons. We could do nothing in the face of that monster you were driving. You ranged up and down the streets, smashing the fronts of buildings, running people down, and laughing. We had to wait until you got off the machine, and then we overpowered you. You were totally mad. It was," he added thoughtfully, "a very interesting study."

"Why did I do it?" I whispered. "How could I do such things to—*you?*"

"You had been hurt. Dreadfully hurt. You had come here, arriving somewhere near this spot. You were crazed by what you had endured. Later, we followed the tracks of your machine back. We found where you had driven it aimlessly over the desert, and where, once you had left the machine and lived in a cave, probably for weeks. You ate desert grasses and the eight-legged crabs. You killed everything you could, through some strange, warped revenge motivation.

"You were crazed with thirst and revenge, and you were very thin, and your face was covered with hair, of all extraordinary things, though analysis showed that you had a constant desire for a hairless face. After treatment you became almost rational. But your time-sense was almost totally destroyed. And you had two almost unbreakable psychological blocks—your memory of how you came here, and your sense of identity.

"We did what we could for you, but you were unhappy. The moons had an odd effect on you. We have two, one well inside the other in its orbit, but both with the same period. Without instruments they appear to be in eclipse when they are full. The sight of what you called that crooked moon undid a lot of our work. And then you would get the attacks of an overwhelming emotion you term 'remorse,' which appeared to be something like cruelty and something like love and included a partial negation of the will to survive . . . and you could not understand why we would not punish you. Punish you—when you were sick!"

"Yes," I said. "I—remember most of it now. You gave me everything I could want. You even gave me—gave me—"

"Oh—that. Yes. You had some deepseated convictions about love, and marriage. We felt you would be happier—"

"I was, and then I wasn't. I—I wanted—"

"I know. I know," he said soothingly. "You wanted your name again, and somehow you wanted your own earth."

I clenched my fists until my forearms hurt. "I should be satisfied," I cried. "I should be. You are all so kind, and she—and she—she's been—" I shook my head angrily. "I must be crazy."

"You generally ask me," he said smiling, "at this point, how you came here."

"I do?"

"You do. I'll repeat it. You see, there are irregularities in the fabric of space. No—not space, exactly. We have a word for it—" (he spoke it) "—which means, literally, 'space which is time which is psyche.' It is a condition of space which by its nature creates time and thought and matter. Your world, relative to ours, is in the infinitely great, or in the infinitely small, or perhaps in the infinitely distant, either in space or in time—it does not matter, for they are all the same thing in their ultimate extensions . . . but to go on:

"While you were at your work, you ran your machine into a point of tension in this fabric—a freak, completely improbable position in—" (he spoke the word again) "—in which your universe and ours were tangential. You—went through."

I tensed as he said it.

"Yes, that was the thing. It caused you inconceivable agony. It drove you mad. It filled you full of vengeance and fear. Well, we—cured you of everything but the single fear of going through that agony again, and the peculiar melancholy involving the loss of your ego— your desire to know your own name. Since we failed there—" he shrugged "—we have been doing the only thing left to us. We are trying to send you back."

"Why? Why bother?"

"You are not content here. Our whole social system, our entire philosophy, is based on the contentment of the individual. So we must do what we can . . . in addition, you have given us a tremendous amount of research material in psychology and in theoretical cosmogony. We are grateful. We want you to have what you want. Your fear is great. Your desire is great- er. And to help you achieve your desire, we have put you on this course of abreaction."

"Abreaction?"

He nodded. "The psychological re-enactment, or retracing, of everything you have done since you came here, in an effort to return you to the entrance-point in exactly the same frame of mind as that in which you came through it. We cannot find that point. It has something to do with your particular psychic matrix. But if the point is still here, and if, by hypnosis, we can cause you to do exactly what you did when you first came through—why, then, you'll go back."

"Will it be—dangerous?"

"Yes," he said, unhesitatingly. "Even if the point of tangency is still here, where you emerged, it may not be the same point on your earth. Don't forget—you have been here for eleven of your years. . . . And then there's the agony—bad enough if you do go through, infinitely worse if you do not, for you may drift in— in *somewhere* forever, quite conscious, and with no possibility of release.

"You know all this, and yet you still want us to try. . . ." He sighed. "We admire you deeply, and wonder too; for you are the bravest man we have ever known. We wonder most particularly at your culture, which can produce such an incredible regard for the ego. . . . Shall we try again?"

I looked at the sun which was too orange, and at the hills, and at his broad, quiet, beautiful face. If I could have spoken my name then, I think I should have stayed. If I could have seen *her* just at that moment, I think I should have waited a little longer, at least.

"Yes," I said. "Let's try it again."

I was so afraid that I couldn't remember my name or the name of Gracias de Nada, or something, the fellow who drove the bottom-dump. I couldn't remember how to run the machine; but my hands remembered, and my feet.

Now I sat and looked at the windrow; and then I pulled back the throttle and raised the blade. I swung into the windrow, and the gravel loaded clean onto the blade and cleanly ran off in two even rolls at the sides. When I sensed that the gravel was all off the blade, I stopped, shifted into high reverse, pulled the left steering clutch to me, let in the master clutch, stamped the left brake. . . .

That was the thing, then. Back-blading that roll out —the long small windrow of gravel that had run off the ends of my blade. As I backed over it, the machine straddling it, I dropped the blade on it and floated it, so that it smoothed out the roll. Then it was that I looked back—force of habit, for a bulldozer that size can do real damage backing into powerpoles or buildings—and I saw the muzzy bit of fill.

It was a patch of spread gravel that seemed whirling, blurred at the edges. Look into the sun and then suddenly at the floor. There will be a muzzy patch there, whirling and swirling like that. I thought something funny had happened to my eyes. But I didn't stop the machine, and then suddenly I was in it.

Again.

It built up slowly, the agony. It built up in a way that promised more and then carefully fulfilled the promise, and made of the peak of pain a further promise. There was no sense of strain, for everything was poised and counter-balanced and nothing would break. All of the inner force was as strong as all the outer forces, and all of me was the point of equilibrium.

Don't try to think about it. Don't try to imagine for a second. A second of that, unbalanced, would crush you to cosmic dust. There were years of it for me; years and years. . . . I was in an unused stockpile of years, somewhere in a hyperspace, and the weight of them all was on me and in me, consecutively, concurrently.

I woke up very slowly. I hurt all over, and that was an excruciating pleasure, because the pain was only physical.

I began to forget right away.

A company doctor came in and peeped at me. I said, "Hi."

"Well, well," he said, beaming. "So the flying cat-skinner is with us again."

"What flying catskinner? What happened? Where am I?"

"You're in the dispensary. You, my boy, were working your bulldozer out on the fill and all of a sudden took it into your head to be a flying kay-det at the same time. That's what they say, anyhow. I do know that there wasn't a mark around the machine where it lay—not for sixty feet. You sure didn't drive it over there."

"What are you talking about?"

"That, son, I wouldn't know. But I went and looked myself. There lay the Cat, all broken up, and you beside it with your lungs all full of your own ribs. Deadest looking man I ever saw get better."

"I don't get it. Did anybody see this happen? Are you trying to—"

"Only one claims to have seen it was a Puerto Rican bottom-dump driver. Doesn't speak any English, but he swears on every saint in the calendar that he looked back after dumping a load and saw you and twenty tons of bulldozer *forty feet in the air,* and then it was coming down!"

I stared. "Who was the man?"

"Heavy-set fellow. About forty-five. Strong as a rhino and seemed sane."

"I know him," I said. "A good man." Suddenly, then, happily: "Doc—you know what his name is?"

"No. Didn't ask. Some flowery Spanish moniker, I guess."

"No, it isn't," I said. "His name is Kirkpatrick. Alonzo Padin de Kirkpatrick."

He laughed. "The Irish are a wonderful people. Go to sleep. You've been unconscious for nearly three weeks."

"I've been unconscious for eleven years," I said, and felt foolish as hell because I hadn't meant to say anything like that and couldn't imagine what put it into my head.

NIGHTMARE ISLAND

The governor took a sight between two leaves of carefully imported mint, lining the green notch up with the corner of the bamboo veranda and the bowed figure of the man on the beach. He was silent so long that his guest became restless, missing the easy drone of the governor's voice. That was the only thing to do, he thought, watching the old man pressing the cool glass against his cheek, peering through the leaves at the beachcomber; the only thing a man could do in this dreary, brilliant group of little islands—you could only talk. If you didn't keep a conversation going, you thought of the heat and the surf-etched silences, and the weary rattle of palm fronds, and that brought you back to the heat again. God, he thought suddenly, the governor dresses for dinner in this heat, every last damn day.

"Poor crazy devil," muttered the governor.

His American visitor asked, "Who?"

The governor gestured with his glass toward the sea and the beachcomber, and then sipped.

The American swiveled and stared. The beachcomber stood dejectedly with the surf tumbling about his knees, and the sun was sinking so rapidly that his shadow crept and crawled along the beach like something with a life of its own. A trick of the light seemed to make the man's flesh transparent for a split second, and it appeared to the American that the man was a broad-shouldered skeleton standing there staring out to sea. A slight shift of shades showed him up again for what he was, the thin husk of a man, sharp-boned, stringy.

The American grunted and turned back toward his host. "What's the matter with him?"

The governor said, "Him? He just doesn't give a damn any more. He lost something and he can't—I can't let him—get it back."

"What did he lose?"

The governor regarded him gravely. "You're a businessman. You deal in dollars and cents and tons— You wouldn't believe me if I told you, and you might not let me finish."

The American opened his mouth to protest, but the governor held up his hand and said, "Listen to that."

The beachcomber's cracked wail drifted out over the cluttered beach and the whispering surf. "Ahniroo!" he cried. "Ahni—Ahniroo!" Then for a long while he was silent, and it grew darker. Just as the sleepy sun pulled the blanket of horizon over its head, they saw the beachcomber's shoulders slump. He turned and walked up the beach.

The American squinted at him. "I take it he isn't as crazy as he looks?"

The governor shook his head. "You can put it that way."

The American settled himself more comfortably. He didn't care about the 'comber particularly, or the governor either, for that matter. But he had to stay here another forty-eight hours, and there would be nothing to do until the mail steamer came except to sit and talk with the old boy. The man seemed to have at least one good yarn to tell, which was promising.

"Come on—give," he grinned. "I'll take your word for it. Don't forget, I'm not used to this kind of country, or the funny business that goes on in it. Who is he, anyhow? And why is he calling out over the water? Gives me the creeps. Who's Ahniroo—or what is it?"

The governor leaned back and looked up at a spider that would probably drop down someone's collar before the evening was over, and he said nothing for quite a while. Then he began:

Ahniroo was a . . . a friend of the fellow's. I doubt that any man has had a friend like that. As far as the man himself is concerned—yes, you may be right. Perhaps he isn't quite all there. But after what he went through, the surprising thing is that he can talk fairly sensibly. Of course, he's peculiar there, too—all he'll talk about is Ahniroo, but he does it quite rationally.

He was a seaman, much like any other seaman. He had relatives ashore and was going to marry one of these years, perhaps; and there was a visit to the place where he was born, some day, when he could walk into the town with a hundred-dollar bill in every pocket of a new suit. Like other seamen he saved his money and spent it and lost it and had it stolen from him, and like some other seamen he drank.

Being on the beach really started the whole thing for him. A sailor's unemployment is unlike any other kind, in that it is so little dependent on the man's whereabouts. A silkmill worker must starve around a silk mill before he can get his job, but a seaman can starve anywhere. If he is a real seaman, he is a painter and a general handyman, a stevedore and roustabout.

Chances are that he can drive a truck or play a little music or can turn his hand at any of a thousand semi-skilled trades. He may not know where he will eat next, but he can always find a bit of drink to warm him or cool him as the weather dictates. But Barry—our beachcomber over there—didn't care much for eating, and didn't do much of it for quite a while, except when it was forced on him. He concentrated on the drinking, and the more he drank the more reasons he found for drinking, until he couldn't walk or sleep or work or travel or stay still without a little snort or two as a persuader. Not so good. He lost a lot of jobs ashore and afloat. When he had a job he'd guzzle to celebrate, and when he lost one he'd guzzle to console himself. You can imagine what happened.

It hit him in a small town on the Florida coast. He had just been fired from a little four-thousand ton freighter that ran coastwise and found that stopping in such half-forgotten whistle stops paid expenses. It was on the North American continent, but aside from that it hardly differed from these islands. It was hot and humid and a long, long way from anywhere else.

And Barry found himself sitting on the edge of a wooden sidewalk with his feet and his soul in the gutter, with no money and no job and no food in his stomach. He felt pretty good, being just halfway between a binge and a hangover. He stared for twenty minutes at a painted stone in the dusty road, just because his eyes happened to be directed that way. And before long a scorpion crept out from behind the stone and stood looking at him.

It was like no other scorpion he had ever seen. It was no larger than any other, and the same dark color, but instead of the formidable pincers, it had *arms*. They were tiny and perfect and pink and soft, and had delicate hands and little diamond specks of fingernails. And—oh, yes, no joints, apparently. They were as sinous as an elephant's trunk. It was such an unheard-of-thing to see that Barry stared at it for a long moment before he let himself believe what he had seen. Then he shook himself, shrugged drunkenly, and said:

"I'll be damned!" And then, addressing the strange scorpion, "Hi!"

The scorpion waved one of its perfect, impossible arms, and said, "You will be!" and then, "Hi yourself."

Barry started so violently that he came to his feet. The liquor he had been sopping seemed to have collected in his knees; at any rate, those members were quite liquid and buckled under him, so that he fell on his face. He remembered the scorpion scuttling away, and then his forehead struck the painted stone and the lights went out for him.

Barry had been a strong man, but after two years of nursing from flat bottles, you wouldn't have known it. He was no beauty. He had a long leather face and purple nose. His eyes were nearly as red as their lids, and his broad shoulders were built of toothpicks and parchment. Skin that had been taut with the solid muscle under it was now loose and dry, and fitted him as badly as the clothes he wore. He was a big fellow—six feet three at least, and he weighed all of a hundred and twenty-seven pounds.

The scorpion was the start of it, and the crack on the skull brought it on full strength. That's right—the horrors. The good old creeping, crawling horrors. When he came to and hauled his ragged body back up to the sidewalk, he found himself in a new world, horribly peopled by things he couldn't understand. There were soft white wriggling things—a carpet of them under his feet. Standing at bay in the doorway of a general store down the street was a gryphon, complete with flaming breath, horns and tail, frighteningly real, lifted bodily from an old book that had frightened him when he was a child. He heard a monstrous rustle over his head; and there was a real life prototype of Alice-in-Wonderland's buck-toothed Jabberwock, and it was out to get him. He shrieked and tried to run, and fell choking and splattering into the Slough of Despond from "Pilgrim's Progress." There was a someone else in there with him—a scantily clad girl on skis from the front cover of a Paris magazine. She laughed and turned into a six-legged winged snake which bit at him viciously and vanished. He scrambled to his feet and plunged sobbing down the dusty road, and people on the sidewalks turned and stared and said, "Crazy with th' heat," and went on about their business, for heat madness was common among beached sailors in August.

Barry staggered on out of town, which wasn't very far, and out among the sand dunes and scrub and saw grass. He began to see things that he could not describe, devils and huge spiders and insects. In the angry blaze of the sun he slumped to his knees, sobbing, and then something clicked in his mind and he collapsed from sheer psychic exhaustion.

It was night, and very cool, when he woke again. There was half a moon and a billion stars, and the desertlike dunes were all black velvet and silver. The black and the gleam were crowded with strange life, but it was worse now than it had been in the daytime, because now he could feel what he couldn't see. He *knew* that twenty feet away from him stood a great foul buzzard that stared steadily at him, and yet he could not see it. It was more than a fearsome sensation that the thing was there; he could feel each feather, every wrinkle of the crusted, wattled neck, each calloused serration on its dry yellow legs. As he stared tremblingly into the mounding distances, he felt the grate of a bison's hoof as it eyed him redly, ready to charge. The sound of a wolf's teeth impacted on his skin rather than his eardrums, and he felt its rough tongue on its black lips. He screamed and ran toward the town, guided by his omnipresent seaman's instinct, dodging and zigzagging among the silver dunes. Oh, yes—he had 'em. He had the horrors really thoroughly.

He reached town about eleven at night. He was pretty much of a mess—covered with grime, cut and bruised and sick. Someone saw him leaning rockily against the sundried wall of a gin mill, trying to revive himself with the faint clinking of glasses and the fainter odor of liquor that drifted from inside. Someone else said, "Look at the hulk; let's feed him a drink." It was a lucky break for Barry; with his metabolism in the pickled state it was, he would most certainly have dropped dead if he had not had that snifter.

They led him in and gave him a couple more, and his garbled mutterings were amusing to them for a time, but after a while they went home and left him cluttering up a round table with his spent body.

Closing time—which meant the time when there was no one left around to buy a nickel beer—came, and the bartender, a misplaced Louisiana Cajun, came over to throw the sailor out. There was no one else in the place but a couple of rats and some flies. One of the rats had only two legs and wore a collar and tie even in that heat. The other rat had some self-respect and scuttled under the beer pulls to lap suds, being a true quadruped with inherited rat reflexes.

The two-legged rat's name was Zilio. He was a small oily creature with swarthy skin, a hooked nose supported by a small mustache, an ingratiating manner and a devious way of making a living. His attention was attracted toward Barry by the barkeep's purposeful approach. Zilio slid off his stool and said:

"Hold it, Pierre; I'm buying for the gentleman. Pour a punch."

The name did not refer to the ingredients of the drink but to its effect. The barkeep shrugged and went back to his bar, where he poured a double drink of cheap whiskey, adding two drops of clear liquid from a small bottle, this being the way to mix a Zilio punch.

Zilio took it from him and carried it over to Barry. He set it on the table in front of the seaman, drew up a chair and sat close to him, his arm on Barry's shoulder.

"Drink up, old man," he said in an affected accent. He shook Barry gently, and the sailor raised his head groggily. "Go on," urged Zilio.

Barry picked up the glass, shaking and slopping, and sipped because he had not energy for a gulp.

"You're a sailor, eh?" murmured Zilio.

Barry shook his head and reared back to try to focus his disobedient eyes on the oily man. "Yeah, an' a damn good one."

"Union member?"

"What's it to you?" asked Barry belligerently, and Zilio pushed the glass a little closer. Barry realized that the smooth, swarthy character was buying a drink, and promptly loosened up. "Yeah; I belong to the union." He picked up the glass.

"Good!" said Zilio. "Drink up!"

Barry did. The raw liquid slid down his throat, looped around and smashed him on the back of the neck. He sank tinglingly into unconsciousness. Zilio watched him for a moment, smiling.

Pierre said, "What are you going to do with that broken down piece o' tar?"

Zilio began to search Barry's pockets diligently. "If I can find what I'm looking for," he said, "this broken down piece of tar is going to be removed from the rolls of the unemployed. Another minute's searching uncovered Barry's seaman's papers. "Ah—able seaman —quartermaster—wiper and messman. He'll do." He stood back and wiped his hands on a large white handkerchief. "Pierre, get a couple of the boys and have this thing brought down to my dock."

Pierre grunted and went out, returning in a few minutes with a couple of fishermen. Without a word they picked up the unconscious Barry and carried him out to a disreputable old flivver, which groaned its way out of sight down the dusty road.

Zilio said, " 'Night, Pierre." He handed the bartender two clean dollar bills for his part in the shanghai, and left.

When Barry swam up out of the effects of Pierre's Mickey Finn, he found himself in all too familiar surroundings. He didn't have to open his eyes; his nose and sense of touch told him where he was. He was lying in a narrow bed, and the sparse springs beneath him vibrated constantly. His right side felt heavier than his left, and he rolled a little that way, and then the weight shifted and he rolled back. He groaned. How did he ever get working again?

He opened his eyes at last, to see what kind of a box

it was that he had shipped out on. He saw a dimly lit fo'c's'le with six bunks in it, only one of which was occupied. The place was filthy, littered with empty beer cans, dirty socks, a couple of pairs of dungarees, wrapping paper from laundry parcels, and cigarette butts—the usual mess of a merchant ship's crew's quarters when leaving port. He closed his eyes and shook his head violently to rid himself of this impossible vision—he didn't remember catching a ship, *knew* he was on the beach, and was good and sick of seeing things he could not believe. So—he closed his eyes and shook his head to clear it, and when he did that he groaned in agony at the pain that shot through it. Oooh—that must have been a party. Wow! He lay very still until the pain subsided, and then cautiously opened his eyes again. He was still in a ship's fo'c's'le.

"Hey!" he called weakly.

The figure on the lower bunk opposite started, and a man pushed his head into the light that trickled in from the alleyway.

"Hey, where am I? Eh—when is this?"

Apparently the man could make sense out of the vague question. "Tuesday," he said. That meant nothing to Barry. "Ye're aboard th' *Jesse Hanck*. Black oil. Far East."

Barry lay back. "Oh," he moaned.

The Hanck ships were famous—or was it notorious? They were old Fore River ships, well-deck tankers. They were dirty and unseaworthy, and they were hungry ships and paid ordinary seamen's wages to their petty officers, grading it on down from there. Twenty-eight lousy dollars a month. No overtime. Eighty-six-day runs.

Barry got up on one elbow and said half to himself, "What did I do—*ask* for this job?"

The other man rolled out and sat on the edge of his bunk, putting on tankerman's safety shoes. "Dam-fino. Did you ever meet a guy called Zilio?"

"Ah— Yeh."

The man nodded. "There you are then, shipmate. He gave you a drink. You passed out. You wake up aboard this oil can. That's Zilio's business."

"Why the dirty— I'm a union member! I'll tie this ship up! I'll have her struck! I'll report her to the Maritime Commission! I'll—"

The other man rose and came across the fo'c's'le to lean his elbows on Barry's bunk and breathe his gingivitis into Barry's face. "You'll do your work and shut up. When you sober up enough to look around, you'll find out you're sailing without seaman's papers. If you're a good boy and play along with the seahorse that calls himself a chief mate, you'll get them back. Step off the straight and narrow and you'll be beached somewhere without your livin'. An' listen—better dry up with that union talk. You got picked up by a fink-herder and shipped on a fink ship. They don't go for that around here, that fellow-worker stuff."

"Yeah?" Barry swung his feet over the side of the bunk and had to clutch his pounding head. "I'll jump ship in Panama! We got to go through the canal!"

"Ain't nobody jumpin' no ship in Panama nowadays, friend. They'll send out a fifth-colyum alarm fer you from the ship an' you'll spend somethin' like fifty years in a military bastille. Besides—time you get to Colon you won't want to be jumpin' ship. Better cool off now. G'wan back to sleep. I got the eight to twelve. You got the twelve to four."

So Barry went to work again. He spent his days and nights in the utmost misery. The packing around the posthole beside his bunk had kicked out some years ago, and every time the weather got a little drafty, his bunk shipped water. The food was atrocious, and the crew was composed of bootblacks, kids on vacation, ex-tenant farmers, and one or two bona-fide seamen like himself, either outright finks or shanghaied wrecks. But all of this didn't stack up to his horrors. They persisted and they grew.

It isn't often a man gets them that badly, but then it isn't often that a man lets himself get into the state that Barry was in. He walked in a narrowing circle of ravenous beasts. When he slept he dreamed horrible dreams, and when he lay awake he could feel tiny, cold, wet feet crawling over his body. He was afraid to stand a lookout watch by himself, and the mate had to batten down his ears for him before he would go out to the fo'c's'le head at night. He was dead sure that there was something horrible hiding in the anchor engine, ready to leap out at him and wrap him up in the anchor cables. He was just as afraid to be in a roomful of men, because, to his sodden eyes, their faces kept running together fluidly, assuming the most terrifying shapes. So he spent his hours off watch hovering in the outskirts of small groups of men, making them nervous, causing them to call him Haunt and Jonah.

He found out what the eight-to-twelve man had meant when he'd said that Barry wouldn't feel like jumping ship in Panama. A day before they made the canal, those who might make trouble were called to the second mate's room, each secretly, and fed rotgut liquor. They hadn't learned—not one of them. It was a Mickey again. When they came to, they were in the Pacific.

The *Jesse Hanck* steamed well out of the usual

steamer lanes. The Hanck fleet were charter boats, and they saw to it that they were always behind schedule sufficiently to enable the captains to pad the fuel and store consumption accounts enough so that pockets were lined all around, except for those of the crews. A thoroughly rotten outfit. At any rate, Barry had his little accident eight days out of the canal.

The ship was shuffling along somewhere on the tenth meridian, and it was hot. It was one of those evenings when a man puts clothes on to soak up perspiration and rips them off thirty seconds later because he can't stand the heat of them; when sleeping on deck is just as bad.

The men bunked all over the place, throwing mattresses down on the after boat deck, swinging hammocks from the midship rigging, crawling under the messroom tables, which were out on the poop now—sleeping anywhere and everywhere in impossible attempts to escape the cruel heat. Calling the watch was a hit-or-miss proposition; you might find your relief and then again you might wake the wrong man from a rare snatch of real sleep and get yourself roughed up for your mistake.

Barry came off watch at four that morning. He turned in somewhere back aft. He never got up for breakfast anyway, and when the eight-to-twelve ordinary seaman tried to call him for lunch at eleven-thirty, he couldn't be found. It was one-thirty before the bos'n missed him. Sometime between four in the morning and one in the afternoon, then, Barry had left the ship.

It gave all hands something to talk about for a couple of days. The captain wrote up a "lost at sea" item in the log and pocketed Barry's wages. An ordinary seaman was given Barry's duties with no increase in pay. Barry was forgotten. Who cared, anyway? Nobody liked him. He wasn't worth a damn. He couldn't steer. He couldn't paint. He was a lousy lookout.

Barry himself always gets that part of his story garbled. How a man trained at sea, capable in any emergency of looking out for his own skin, no matter what the weather or his state of sobriety, could possibly *fall* off a ship at sea is beyond understanding. I don't believe he did. I think he jumped off. Not because of the way he was being treated aboard that slave ship; he hadn't self-respect enough left for that. It must have been his horrors; at any rate, that, according to him, is the last thing he remembers happening to him aboard the *Jesse Hanck*.

He had just drifted off to sleep, when he was aroused by some shipboard noise—the boilers popping off, perhaps, or a roar from the antiquated steering engine. At any rate, he was suddenly dead certain that something was pursuing him, and that if he didn't get away from it, he would be horribly killed. He tried, and then he was in the water.

As the rusty old hull slid past him in the warm sea, he looked up at it and blinked the brine out of his failing eyes and made not the slightest attempt to shout for help. He trod water for some moments, until the after light of the tanker was a low star swinging down on the horizon, and then he turned over on his back and kicked sluggishly to keep himself afloat.

Now delirium tremens is a peculiar affliction. Just as the human body can be destroyed by a dose of poison, but will throw off an overdose, so the human mind will reach a point of supersaturation and return to something like normality. In Barry's case it was a pseudosanity; he did not cease to have his recurrent attacks of phantasmagoria, but he became suddenly immunized to them. It was as if he had forgotten how to be afraid—how, even, to wonder at the things he saw and felt. He simply did not care; he became as he is today, just not giving a damn. In effect, his mind was all but completely gone, so that for the first time in weeks he could lie at ease and feel that he was not mortally afraid. It was the first time he had been in real danger, and he was not afraid.

He says that he lay there and slept for weeks. He says that porpoises came and played with him, bunting him about and crying like small children. And he says that an angel came down from the sky and built him a boat out of seaweed and foam. But he only remembers one sun coming up, so it must have been that same morning that he found himself clutching a piece of driftwood, rocking and rolling in a gentle swell just to windward of a small island. It was just a little lump of sand and rock, heaped high in the middle, patched with vegetation and wearing a halo of shrieking sea birds. He stared at it with absolutely no interest at all for about four hours, drifting closer all the while. When his feet struck bottom he did not know what it meant or what he should do; he just let them drag until his knees struck also, and then he abandoned his piece of wood and crept ashore.

The sun was coming up again when Barry awoke. He was terribly weak, and his flesh was dry and scaly the way only sea-soaked skin can be. His tongue was interfering with his breathing. He lolled up to his hands and knees and painfully crawled up the sloping beach to a cluster of palms. He collapsed with his chin in a cool spring, and would have killed himself by over-drinking if he had not fallen asleep again.

The next time he pushed the groggy clouds from him, he felt much better. He was changed; he knew that. He was basically changed; he felt different about things. It took him quite a while to figure out just how, but then it occurred to him that though he was still surrounded with the monsters and visions and phantoms of his own drink-crazed creation, he did not fear them. But it was more than that. It was not the disinterest he had experienced out there when he was adrift. It was a sullen hatred of the things. It was an eagerness to have one of them come near enough for him to attack. He crouched by the spring and looked craftily about him, crying to find an object to kill and tear. He found it. Near him was a coconut. He picked up a stone and hurled it, and cracked the coconut. He caught it up and drank greedily from the streaming cracks, and then broke it and ate the meat until it made him sick. He was enormously pleased with himself.

All around him the ground pimpled and dimpled, and from the little depressions what he thought were strange plants began to grow. They were sinuous stalks, and they seemed to be made of two rubbery sheaths that wound about each other spirally, forming a tentaclelike stem, and spreading out at the tip in two flashy extensions like snail's eyes. He reached out and touched one as it grew visibly, and it writhed away from him and began clubbing the ground blindly, searchingly. He'd never dreamed up anything like this before. But he was certain he had nothing to fear from them. He got up, kicking one out of the

way disgustedly, and began to climb the central hill
for bearings. Just as he left, one of the growths spurted
up out of the ground, curved over his head and
smashed wetly down on the spot he had just vacated.
He didn't even look over his shoulder. Why should
he, for a figment of his imagination? The mistake he
made was that the things were real. Just as real, my
friend, as you and I!

Barry, poor crazed wreck, couldn't realize it then,
because the growing, writhing trunks all around him
were mixed and mingled with things of his own
creation, dancing and gibbering around him. There
were things harmless and beautiful, and things too
foul to mention, and it is little wonder that the
stemlike things were of little importance.

Barry went on up the hill. He picked up a thorny
stick, quite heavy, and strode on, casually swiping
at his monsters, real and imaginary. He noticed sub-
consciously that when he struck at a unicorn or a
winged frog, it would vanish immediately, but when
he swung at a growing tentacle it would either duck
quickly or, when struck, twist into a tight knot about
its wound. He even looked back and noticed how
the stalks kept pace with him, sinking back into the
ground behind him and sprouting ahead. It still
meant nothing to him.

A few hundred yards from the top he stopped and
sniffed. There had been a growing, fetid odor about
the place, and he didn't like it. He connected it somehow with the smell of the ichor that exuded from
the wounded stalks after he had slashed them, but he
was incurious; he didn't really care. He shrugged
and finished his climb.

When he had reached the top he stood a moment

wiping his forehead with his wrist, and then sighted all around the horizon. There were no other islands in sight. This one was small—nearly round, and perhaps a mile by a mile and a quarter. He spotted two more springs and a tight grove of coconut and breadfruit. That was encouraging. He stepped forward as a rubbery trunk poured out of the ground and lashed at his legs with its two prehensile tentacles. It missed.

A puff of wind bearing an unspeakable odor brought his attention back to the crest of the hill. It was nearly round, almost exactly following the contours of the island, and fell in the center to form a small crater. Down at the bottom of the crater was a perfectly round hole, and that was the source of the noisome smell.

Barry walked down toward it because he happened to be facing that way and it was the easiest way to go. He was halfway down the slope when two points of what looked like pulpy flesh began to rise out of the hole. They seemed to be moving slowly, but Barry suddenly realized that it was an illusion due to their enormous size. Before he could bring himself to stop, they had risen twenty feet in the air. They began leaning outward, one directly toward him, the other across the hole, away from him. They grew thicker as they poured upward and outward, and finally they lay flat on the slope and the near one began licking up toward him.

It was the most frightening phantasm that had yet presented itself to Barry's poor alcoholic brain, but now he would not be frightened. He stood there, legs apart, club at the ready, and waited. When the thing reached his feet he raised himself on his toes and brought the thorny club down with all his strength

on its fleshy tip. It winced away and then poured
back. He hit it twice more and it retreated. He ran
after it and smashed it again and again. It suddenly
rocketed up in the air, as did its mate from the other
side of the crater. They struck together with a mighty
wet *smack!* and stood there, a pale-green, shining
column of living flesh, quivering in the sunlight. And
then, with unbelievable speed, they plunged into the
ground, back into their hole. Barry dropped his club,
clasped his hands over his head and smirked. Then
he turned and went back to his spring.

And all the way back, not another trunk showed
itself.

He slept well that night under a crude shelter of
palm leaves. Not a thing bothered him but dreams,
and of course they didn't bother him much any
more. His victory over the thing in the crater had
planted a tiny seed of self-esteem in that rotten hulk
of a man. That, added to the fact that he was too
crazy to be afraid of anything, made him something
new under the sun.

In the morning he sat up abruptly. At his feet
was a pile of breadfruit and coconuts, and around
him was a forest, a wall of the waving stalks. He
leaped to his feet and cast about wildly for his club.
It had disappeared. He drew his sheath knife, which
by some miracle had stayed with him since he left the
Jesse Hanck, and stood there, palisaded by the thickly
planted, living stems. And he still was not afraid. He
took a deep breath and stepped menacingly toward
the near wall of stalks. They melted into the ground
before he reached them. He whirled and rushed those
behind him. They were gone before he could get
within striking distance. He paused and nodded to

himself. If that was the way they wanted it, it was
O.K. He put away his knife and fell to on the fruit.
The stems ranked themselves at a respectful distance,
as if they were watching. And then he noticed something new. Deep within his brain was a constant,
liquid murmur, as if thousands of people were talking quietly together in a strange tongue. He didn't
mind it very much. He'd been through worse, and he
wasn't curious.

After he was quite finished he noticed a rustling
movement in the wall surrounding him. The creatures
were passing something, one to the other—his club!
It reached the stalk nearest him; it was taken and
laid gently by his side. The stalk straightened and
dropped into the earth quickly as if it were embarrassed.

Barry looked at the waving things and almost
grinned. Then he picked up the club. Immediately
the things on one side of him melted into the ground,
and those on the other side doubled in number. A
couple of them began sprouting under his feet; he
jumped away, startled. More sank into the earth
from his path, and more sprang up behind. He looked
at them a little uneasily; it occurred to him that they
were a little insistent, compared with his usual disappearing monsters. He walked away from them. They
followed; that is, they massed behind him, sprouting
in his footsteps. And the murmuring in his mind
burst into a silent cacophony; gleeful, triumphant.

He wandered inland, followed by his rustling company of pale-green stalks. When he turned aside they
would spring up around him and it was no good
trying to press through. They made no attempt to
harm him at all. But—they were *forcing* him toward
the hill! Perhaps he realized it—perhaps not. Barry,

by this time, was totally unhinged. Any other man could not have lived through what he did. But his peculiar conditioning, the subtle distortion of his broken mind, gave him the accidental ability to preserve himself. Certainly he himself could take no credit for it. His fantastic world was no more strange to him than ours is to us. If you or I were suddenly transported to that island, we would be as frightened as—well, a gorilla in Times Square, or a New Yorker in the African jungle. It's all a matter of receptivity.

And so he found himself marching up the central slope, being driven gently but firm toward that monstrous thing in the crater by his entourage of pale-green stalks. They must have been a weird-looking company.

And the thing was waiting for him. He came up over the crest of the rise, and the tip of one of the two great green projections curled up over his head and lashed down at him. He threw himself sideways and belted it with his club as it touched the ground. It slid back toward the hole. He took a step or two after it. It was huge—fully sixty feet of it stretched from him to the hole in the center of the crater. And no telling how much more of it was in there. At the first movement from the thing, there had been a rustle behind him and every one of the stalks had dropped from sight.

As Barry ran forward to strike again, a shape shot up out of the ground at his side, whipped around his leg and flung him down. He rolled over and sat up, to see the other great green arm come swooping down on the stalk that had tripped him and—saved his life. The two huge tentacles slapped together, twisted the slender stalk between them, and began to pull. The stalk tried to go underground, and for a moment held, while its spiraled body stretched and thinned under tons of pull. Then the ground itself gave, and with a peculiar sucking sound, the stalk came up out of the earth. And for the first time Barry saw it for what it was.

The "root" was a dark-green ovoid, five or six feet long, about two and a half feet thick at the middle. It was rough and wrinkled, and gleamed with its coating of slime. The stalk itself was eight feet long. The creature hung for a moment in the twin tentacles of its captor, and then it was infolded, the bulge of it sliding visibly down the two arms which had closed together and twisted, forming a great proboscis-like tube. And Barry heard it scream, deep down in his mind.

Barry rose and scrambled back over the crest of the hill. It had occurred to him that the monster in the crater had struck at a victim—himself and that the stalk had sacrificed itself to save him. Having a victim, it would be satisfied for the time being. He was right. Peering back, he saw the great column rise in the air and slip swiftly back into its hole. And he realized something else, as the two tips disappeared underground. The divided proboscis—the ability to rise from and sink into the earth—why, the big fellow there was exactly the same as all the rest of these creatures, except for its huge size!

What was it? Why, Barry never knew exactly, and though I took a great deal of trouble to find out, I never bothered to tell him. There they were; more than that, Barry did not care. He still doesn't. However, as closely as I can discover, I think that the creatures were a species of marine worm—one of the *Echiuroidea,* to be exact—*bonellia viridis.* They grow large anywhere they grow, but I've never heard of one longer than four feet, proboscis and all. However, I think it quite possible for a colony to develop in a given locality, and mutate into greater size. As for the big one—well, Barry did find a thing or two out about that monster.

Barry went back down the hill and headed for cover. He wanted to sit somewhere in the shade where he would not be bothered by such things. He found himself a spot and relaxed there. And slowly, then faster and faster, the stalks began to spring up around him again. They kept their distance, almost respectfully; but there was a certain bland insistence in their presence that annoyed Barry.

"Go away!" he said sharply.

And they did. Barry was utterly astonished. It was the first really human reaction that had struck him in weeks. But the sight of these curious creatures, so dissimilar to anything that he had ever heard about, obeying him so implicitly, struck some long-buried streak of humor in the man. He roared with laughter.

"Hello."

His laughter cut off and he peered around. Nothing.

"Hello." The sound seemed to come from no specific direction—as a matter of fact, it seemed to come from no direction at all. It seemed to come from inside him, but he hadn't spoken.

"Who said that?" he snapped.

"I did," said the voice. He looked around again, and his eyes caught a movement down low, to his left. There, just peeping out of the ground, were the twin tendrils that tipped the ubiquitous stalks.

"You?" asked Barry, pointing.

The creature rose another two feet and swayed gently. "Yes."

"And what the hell might you be?"

"I don't understand you. What is hell?"

"It speaks English!" gasped Barry.

"I speak," agreed the monster. "What is English?"

Barry rose to his knees and stared at it. "What are you?" he repeated.

"Man."

"Yeah? What does that make me?"

"You are different. I have only your words for everything. Your name for yourself is Man. My name for myself is Man, too. I have no name for you."

"I'm a man," asserted Barry, half truthfully.

"And what would you say I am?"

Barry looked at it carefully. "A damned nightmare."

The thing said seriously, "Very well. Hereafter we shall be known as nightmares. I shall tell all the people."

The thought of actually having a conversation with this unpleasant-looking beast struck Barry again and almost overwhelmed him. "How the devil can you speak with me?"

"My mind speaks to your mind."

"Yeah? Gee!" was the only comment Barry could think of.

"What are you going to do?" asked the creature.

"Whatcha mean?"

"You have proved yourself against the Big One. We know you can destroy him. Will you do it soon, please?"

"The Big One? You mean that thing in the crater?"

"Yes."

"What can I do?"

"You will know, all-powerful one."

Barry looked around to find out who was being addressed in such prepossessing terms, and then concluded that it was he. He puffed his chest. "Well," he said, "I'll make a deal with you. Get me a drink and I'll fix you up."

It was an old mental reflex, one he had used all over the coast to get himself plastered when offered any kind of a job, aside from shipping out. His technique was to demand more liquor until he was so drunk he was of no value to any kind of an employer; and they would go away and leave him alone.

The stalk said, "It shall be done."

A whirring telepathic signal sounded in Barry's brain, and two or three dozen of the things leaped out of the earth.

"The master desires a drink. And pass the word; hereafter we are to be known as nightmares. It is his wish."

The stalks dropped out of sight, all but the one Barry was talking with.

"Well; that's something like service," breathed Barry.

"All things are yours for the service you will do us," said the nightmare.

"This is the damnedest thing," said Barry, scratching his head. "Why didn't you talk to me before?"

"I did not know what your intentions were, nor whether or not you were an intelligent animal," said the nightmare.

"Y'know now, huh?"

"Yes, master."

"Hey— How come none of 'em talk to me but you?"

"I differ slightly from the rest. See those birds?"

Barry looked up at the wheeling, screaming cloud of gulls and curlews. "So?"

The nightmare gave a peculiar telepathic whistle. The birds wheeled and hurtled downward toward them. In an instant the glade was filled with them. Barry was cuffed and slapped by their wings as they crowded about him. He snatched at a large bird, caught it by the leg, and promptly twisted its neck.

At the nightmare's sudden signal, the rest of the birds turned and fluttered and soared up and away.

"Why did you do that?" asked the nightmare.

"I'm going to eat it."

"You eat birds?"

"Why not?"

"You shall have all you want. But as I was saying—I am different from these others. Of all of us, I alone can call the birds. Apparently, only I may speak with you."

"Seems like. I can—hear the others, but I dunno what they're driving at. What about this Big One. Where'd he come from?"

"The Big One was one of us. But he differed also. He was a mutant, like me, but he is unintelligent. He eats his own kind, which we cannot do. He is very old, and every time he eats one of us, he grows larger. He can't move from the crater because it is rockbound, and he can't burrow through it. But the larger he grows the farther he can reach. If you were not going to kill him, he would grow until he could reach the whole island, or so they say. It used to be, a thousand years ago, that he could travel our roads—"

"Roads? I didn't see no roads."

"Oh, they are underground. The whole island is honeycombed with our burrows. We never put more of ourselves above the surface than our proboscis. We catch our food that way, feeling about the ground and the water's edge for small plants and animals. We can dig, too, almost as fast as we can travel through our roads—Here's your drink."

Barry watched fascinated as a column of stalks approached, bearing gourds of coconut shells filled with water, coconut milk, and breadfruit juice. Never a drop was spilled, as the stalks progressed. Two or three would sprout swiftly, lean back, toward the gourd bearers. They would take the burden, bend swiftly forward and pass it on to some newly sprouted nightmares, and then sink into the ground and appear ahead.

"Why don't they carry it underground?" asked Barry.

"It might not suit you then, master. You live in the sun, and the foods you have eaten have grown in the sun. It shall be as you wish it."

Barry extended his hand and a coconut shell full of cool water was deposited in it. He sipped once and threw it down. "Call this a drink?" he roared. "Get me a *drink*!"

"What would you like?"

"Whiskey, damn you! Gin, rum—beer! Wine, if you can't find anything better." The more he thought of it, the thirstier he got. "Get me a drink, you—what's your name?"

"Ahniroo."

"Well, get it anyway." Barry slumped sullenly back.

"Master—we have none of these things you ask. Could we perhaps make one of them?"

"Make one? I don't—wait a minute." Barry did a little thinking. If he had to make a drink—brew it up, wait for it to ferment, strain it—well, he'd just as soon do without. But it seemed as if these goofy critters were aching to work for him. "O.K.—I'll tell you what to do."

And so Barry gave his orders. He knew very vaguely what to do, purely because he had some idea of what alcoholic drinks were made out of. And it passed the time pleasantly. He had plenty to eat and drink and never had to lift a finger to get it. For the first time in his life he had the kind of existence he'd dreamed about—even if it was mixed up with nightmares.

The base of his brew was coconut milk. He'd heard somewhere that an otherwise innocuous drink would ferment if you put in a raisin and closed the container tightly. No raisins, though. He tried several things and finally got fair results with chunks of breadfruit dried on the rocks in the sun. These were put into a plugged coconut shell, the opening carefully sealed with a whittled wooden stopper and sealed with mucous from the hides of the nightmares. Barry wasn't finicky.

It was a pleasure to watch them work. They co-operated admirably, grouping about a task, each supplying one or both of the "fingers" at the tips of their proboscis. To see a coconut held, plugged, doctored with a breadfruit and sealed up again, was a real pleasure, so swiftly and deftly was it done. Barry had only to whittle one plug when the knife was taken from him and three of the stalks took over the task, one to handle the knife, two to hold the wood. And do you know how many coconuts Barry had them prepare? By actually count, according to Ahniroo—over nine thousand!

And when it was done, Barry announced that it would be, anyway, six months before the stuff was worth drinking. The nightmares, in effect, shrugged that off. They had lots of time. One of them was detailed to mark off the days; and in the meantime they waited on Barry hand and foot. No mention was made of the Big One. And Barry lay and dreamed the days away, thinking of the binge he was going to go on when he could get his hands on nine thousand bottles of home brew!

"Governor," said the American, as the old man stopped to light a cigar, "tell me something. Isn't it a little tough to believe this drunkard's yarn? That business of the worms having intelligence and talking with him. Isn't that a little strong?"

The governor considered. "Perhaps. But once you get over the initial surprise of an idea like that, try taking it apart. Why shouldn't they be intelligent? Just what is intelligence anyway?"

"Why"—the American fingered his Adam's apple uneasily—"I'd say intelligence was what we have that makes us the leading race on the planet."

"Are we, though? We're outnumbered by thousands of other species—worms, for instance, if numbers is your idea of racial supremacy. We are not as strong as the elephant or as quick as the antelope—strength and speed have nothing to do with supremacy. No, we use our intelligence to make tools. We owe our position on earth to our ability to make tools."

"Is that intelligence—tool-making?"

The governor shook his head. "It is one of the ways to use intelligence."

"What about these worms of Barry's, then—why didn't they have cities and literature and machines?"

"They didn't need them. They were not overcrowded on the island. There was plenty to eat for all.

The only menace they had was the Big One, and even that wasn't a complete menace—he could have lived another twenty thousand years without endangering the life of any but those who wandered too close. His presence was a discomfort. As to their literature—how can we know about that? Barry was a seaman, and a very low-type seaman, an ignoramus. What did he care about the splendid brains that Ahniroo and his people might have had? Intelligence of that sort must have produced superb developments along some lines. Barry never bothered to find out.

"No, you can't judge the intelligence of a race by its clothes or its automobiles or its fancy foods. Intelligence is a cellular accident affecting the nervous cysts of certain races. It might strike anywhere. It seems as if it is a beautiful jest handed about by the gods, like a philanthropist giving away beautiful grand pianos to uneducated children. Some may learn to play them. Some may build intricate machines with the parts. Most would destroy them, one way or another. What do you think our race is doing with its great gift? Well?"

The American grinned. "Better get on with your story."

Well, for those six months Barry lived in the lap of luxury. Yes, raw sea birds and coconut and breadfruit and clams can be luxury, once you're used to them. It isn't what you have that makes luxury, anyway; it's how it's given to you. A raw albatross, carefully cleaned and cut up, is as great a luxury when it is brought to you in style as is a twelve-dollar French meal that you have to cook yourself. Barry had nothing to kick about. He had never felt better in his life; he hadn't sense enough to realize that it was largely due to his being on the wagon. He used to dream about coconut shells filled with rare old Scotch now, instead of winged dragons and snakes.

The months went by far faster than he realized; it was a real surprise to him when Ahniroo came to him one morning bearing a coconut.

"It is ready, master."

"What?"

"The drink you asked to have us make for you."

"Oh boy, oh boy! Give it here."

Ahniroo leaned toward him and he took the nut. A jab with his knife drove the plug in, and he took two gulps. One went down and the other went immediately out.

"*Phhhtooey!* Ahni, take this some place and bury it. Holy sweet Sue! It tastes like th' dregs of a city dump!"

Ahniroo took the nut gravely and swayed away. "Yes, master."

Barry sat there running his tongue around the inside of his mouth to get rid of the taste. The tongue moved more and more slowly; he stopped; he swallowed twice, then he leaped to his feet. "Hold it!" he bellowed. "I've drank worse'n that an' paid money for it. Bring that back. Bring fifty of 'em." He snatched the nut and drained it. It was alcoholic, after all. It tasted like nothing on earth, but it had a slight wallop.

Three hours later found Barry sprawled out amid a litter of broken coconut shells. There was a peaceful smile on his long horsy face, and in his mind was unalloyed bliss. Ahniroo bent over and touched the back of his neck with a slimy tentacle. Barry rolled his head and lay still again. Ahniroo was very persistent. Barry finally rolled over and sat up, promptly falling over the other way and lying prone again. Ahniroo and two of his fellows helped to roll him over on his back and sit him up again. Ahniroo shook him gently for some eight minutes until he began to grumble.

"Master—it is time! Come, please; we are waiting."

"Time? What time?"

"Your promise, all-powerful one. We have fulfilled your desire. You promised us you would kill the Big One when we had brought you a drink. You have had your drink, master."

Barry clapped his hand to his brow and winced. Promised? Was that what— Then this wasn't all for nothing? He had to pay off? The full import of it struck him. He was deputized to rid the island of that monstrosity that lived in the crater?

"Now let's be reas'n'ble," he coaxed. "You can't make me do that job, now; y'know y'cant, huh?" Getting no answer from Ahniroo, he said belligerently, "Listen, bean pole, you can't push me around. S'pose I don't even try to do that job?"

Ahniroo said quietly, "You will. You have promised. Come now."

A shrill signal, and Barry found himself lifted bodily and set on his feet. Spluttering and protesting, he was shoved by a solid wall of nightmares toward the hill. Twice he tried to simply quit—sit down, the way he had on the tank ships when he thought he was getting the run-around. The *Echiuroidea* did not understand modern labor methods. They picked him up and carried him when he would not walk. And once he tried to run away. They let him—provided he ran toward the hill. He finally settled to a hesitant plodding, and marched along, wishing the island was ten times as big and he was twenty times smaller.

* * *

When they reached the top of the hill, the nightmares disappeared into the ground, all but Ahniroo. Barry was in tears.

"Ahni—do I hafta?"

"Yes—master."

Barry looked toward the hole. It was sixty feet away and thirty feet in diameter. "Big, ain't he?"

"Very."

"How's about a little drink before I go down there?"

"Of course, master!"

Ahni gave his signal. In a few minutes a stream of coconuts began to pop out of the earth. They were the only thing of Barry's that Ahniroo would allow to be transported underground.

When fifty or sixty had arrived, Barry broke and drained three. "I tell you, Ahni," he said, "just you keep 'em coming. I'll need 'em."

He gave a hitch at his belt and started down the slope, a coconut in each fist. There was no sign at all of the Big One. He walked to the edge of the pit and looked down, trying to hold his breath against the smell of the thing. Yeah—there he was, the little rascal. He could just see the tips of his proboscis.

"C'mon up and fight!" Barry yelled drunkenly.

Still no movement. Barry grinned weakly and looked back toward the edge of the crater. Ahniroo was there, watching. Barry felt a little foolish.

"Come on," he coaxed. "Here; have a drink." He cracked open a coconut and let the fluid run into the pit. There was a stir of movement, and then silence.

Ahni's mental voice came to him. "The Big One is not hungry today."

"Maybe he's thirsty then. Roll me down a couple dozen nuts, pal."

The obedient nightmares shoved at the pile of doctored coconuts. They came rolling and bouncing down the slope. He broke them and pitched them in—about thirty of them. He had not countermanded his order—they were still coming up there.

The Big One thrust up a tentacle, waved it and let it slump back. The last few drinks were getting Barry down. He was long past the stage when he knew what he was doing.

"Hey; My pal wants more! Come on—fill 'em up! He's a big feller—he needs a man-size drink. Couple o' you guys give me a hand!"

Two stalks immediately appeared beside him. He gave no thought to the fact that he was possibly leading them to their deaths. The three began breaking coconut shells and pouring the contents into the pit.

Now just why this happened I could not say. Perhaps the Big One was allergic to alcohol. Perhaps it tripped up his co-ordination so that he couldn't control a movement once it started. But suddenly, with a wheezing roar, the Big One rose up out of his lair.

It is all but impossible to describe that sight. The proboscis alone was fully one hundred and twenty feet long, and it rose straight up in the air, twisting slowly, and then fell heavily to the ground. It lay on the floor of the crater, reaching from the center pit all the way up and over and well down the hill. If it had fallen on Barry it would have crushed him instantly beyond all semblance of a man. And it didn't miss him by much. The two tips of the proboscis were out of sight now, but the whole mass, eighteen feet thick, pulsed and twitched with the violent movement that must have been going on at the extremity.

Barry fell back aghast, in that instant cold sober. Ahniroo's message cut through his awed horror:

"The bristles, master! Cut the bristles!"

Barry drew his knife and ran to the edge of the pit. The actual body of the thing, that thick ovoid part, was just visible, and he could see the bristles—the powerful muscled projections by which the creatures, all of them, burrowed. But the flesh about the Big One's bristles was soft and flabby—it had been decades since he had been able to use them. Barry leaned over and hacked hysterically at the base of one of them. The steel slid through the layers of tissue, and in a moment the bristle hung loose, useless. Barry flung himself aside to avoid a foul gush of ichor, and drove for the other bristle. He couldn't do as much to this one; it sank into the side of the pit, trying to force the great body back into the hole. The earth yielded; the bristle whipped up through the ground and smacked into the Big One's side. That was its last anchorage, and its last refuge was gone.

Immediately the crater was alive with the wavering stems of Ahniroo's kind. Like ants around a slug, they fastened to the gigantic body, dragged and tore at it, tied it to earth. Barry danced around it, his mind drink-crazed again; he waved a full coconut shell aloft in one hand and with the other cut and slashed at the prone monster. He laughed and shrieked and sang, and finally collapsed weakly from sheer exhaustion, still murmuring happily and humming to himself.

Ahniroo and some others carried him back down and laid him on the beach. They washed him and put soft leaves under his body. They fed him continuously out of the huge stock of coconut shells. They almost killed him with kindness. And for his sake, I suppose, they shouldn't have left him on the beach. Because he got—rescued.

*   *   *

A government launch put into the cove to survey, since these days you never can tell what salty little piece of rock might be of military value. They found him there, dead drunk on the beach. It was quite a puzzle to the shore party. There he was, with no footprints around him to show where he'd come from; and though they scoured the neighborhood of the beach, they found no shelter or anything that might have belonged to him. And when they got him aboard and sobered him up the island was miles astern. He went stark raving mad when he discovered where he was. He wanted to go back to his worms. And he's been here ever since. He's no use to anyone. He drinks when he can beg or steal it. He'll die from it before long, I suppose, but he's only happy when he's plastered. Poor devil. I could send him back to his island, I suppose, but— Well, it's quite a problem. Can I, as the representative of enlightened humanity in this part of the world, allow a fellow human being to go back to a culture of worms?

The American shuddered. "I—hardly think so. Ah— governor, is this a true yarn?"

The governor shrugged. "I'll tell you—I was aboard that launch. I was the one who found Barry on the beach. And just before we lost sight of the island, some peculiar prompting led me to look at the beach again through my glasses. Know what I saw there?

"It was *alive*! It was one solid mass of pale-green tentacles, all leaning toward the launch and Barry. There was an air about them—the way they were grouped, their graceful bending toward us—I don't know—that made me think of a prayer meeting. And I distinctly heard—not with my ears, either—'Master, come back! Master!' Over and over again.

"Barry's a god to those damned things. So are the rest of us, I imagine. That's why they were too frightened by us to show themselves when we went ashore there. Ah, poor Barry. I should send him back, I suppose. It's not fair to keep him here—but damn it, I'm a man! I can't cater to a society of— Ugh!"

They sat silently for a long while. Then the American rose abruptly. "Good night, governor. I don't—*like* that story." He smiled wryly and went inside, leaving the old man to sit and stare out to sea.

Late that night the American looked out of his bedroom window uncomfortably. The ground was smoothly covered with a rather ordinary lawn near the governor's house. Farther back, there was night-shadowed jungle.

LARGO

The chandeliers on the eighty-first floor of the Empire State building swung wildly without any reason. A company of soldiers marched over a new, well-built bridge, and it collapsed. Enrico Caruso filled his lungs and sang, and the crystal glass before him shattered.

And Vernon Drecksall composed his Largo.

He composed it in hotel rooms and scored it on trains and ships, and it took more than twenty-two years. He started it in the days when smoke hung over the city, because factories used coal instead of broadcast power; when men spoke to men over wires and never saw each other's faces; when the nations of earth were ruled by the greed of a man or the greed of men. During the Thirty Days War and the Great Change which followed it, he labored; and he finished it on the day of his death.

It was music. That is a silly, inarticulate phrase. I heard a woman say "Thank you" to the doctor who cured her cancer, and then she cried, for the words said so little. I knew a man who was born lonely, and whose loneliness increased as he lived until it was a terrible thing. And then he met the girl he was to marry, and one night he said, "I love you." Just words; but they filled the incredibly vast emptiness within him; filled it completely, so that there was enough left over to spill out in three syllables, eight letters . . . The Largo—it was music. Break away from individual words; separate yourself from the meaning of them strung together, and try to imagine music like Drecksall's Largo in E Flat. Each note was more than polished—burnished. As music is defined as a succession of notes, so the Largo was a thing surpassing music; for its rests, its upbeats, its melodic pauses were silences blended in harmony, in discord. Only Drecksall's genius could give tangible, recognizable tone to silence. The music created scales and keys and chords of silence, which played in exquisite counterpoint with the audible themes.

It was dedicated to Drecksall himself, because he was a true genius, which means that everything in the universe which was not a part of him existed for him. But the Largo was written for Wylie, and inspired by Gretel.

They were all young when they met. It was at a summer resort, one of those strange outposts of city settlement houses. The guests were plumbers and artists and bankers and stenographers and gravicab drivers and students. Pascal Wylie was shrewd and stocky, and came there to squander a small inheritance at a place where people would be impressed by it. He had himself convinced that when the paltry thousands were gone he could ease himself into a position where more could be gotten by someone else's efforts. Unfortunately this was quite true. It is hardly just, but people like that can always find a moneymaker to whom their parasitism is indispensable.

Gretel was one of the students. Without enthusiasm, she attended a school in the city which taught a trade for which she was not fitted and which would not have supported her if she had been. Wylie's feminine counterpart, she was spending her marriageable years, as he spent his money, in places where it would impress others less fortunate. Like him, she lived in a passively certain expectation that when her unearned assets were gone, the future would replace them. Her most valuable possession was a quick smile and a swifter glance, which she used very often—whenever, in fact, a remark was made in her presence which she did not understand. The smile and the glance were humorous and understanding and completely misleading. The subtler the remark, the quicker her reaction. Her rather full lips she held slightly parted, and one watched them to catch the brilliantly wise thought they were about to utter. They never did. She was always surrounded by quasi-sophisticates and pseudo-intellectuals whose conversation got farther and farther above her silly head until she retreated behind one slightly raised golden eyebrow, her whole manner indicating that the company was clever, but a bit below her. She was unbelievably dumb and an utterly fascinating person to know slightly.

Vernon Drecksall washed pots and groomed vegetables for the waspish cook. He had a violin and he cared about little else, but he had discovered that to be able to play he must eat, and this job served to harness his soul to earth, where it did not belong. He got as many dollars each week as he worked hours each day, an arrangement which was quite satisfactory by his peculiar standards.

Each night after Drecksall had scoured the last of his eight dozen pots, disposed of his three bushels of garbage, and swabbed down an acre and a half of floor-space, he went to his room for his violin and then headed for the privacy of distance. Up into the forest on a rocky trail that took him to the brink of a hilltop lake he would go; beating through thick undergrowth he reached a granite boulder that shouldered out into the water at the end of a point. Night after night he stood there on that natural stage and played with almost heartbreaking abandon. Before him stretched the warm, black water, studded with starlight, like the eyes of an audience. Like the glow of an usher's torch, the riding lights of a passing heliplane would move over the water. Like the breathing of twenty thousand spellbound people, the water pressed and stroked and rustled on the bank. But there was never any applause. That suited his mood. They didn't applaud Lincoln at Gettysburg either.

Every ten days the pot-walloper was given a day off, which meant that he worked only until noon, which, again, generally turned out to be four in the afternoon after various emergency odds and ends had been taken care of. Then he had the privilege of circulating among people who disliked him on sight while he mourned that the woods were full of vandals and the lake was full of boats and the telejuke box was incapable of anything but rhythmically insincere approaches to total discord. He didn't look forward to his days off, until he saw Gretel.

She was sitting on an ancient Hammond electric organ, staring off into space, and thinking about absolutely nothing. The mountain sunset streamed through a window behind her, making her hair a halo and her profiled body the only thing in the universe fit to be framed by that glorious light. Drecksall was unprepared for the sight; he was blinded and enslaved. He didn't believe her. She must be music. It was, for him, a perfectly rational conclusion, for she was past all understanding, and until now nothing not musical had struck him that way. He moved over to her and told her so. He was not trying to be poetic when he said, "Someone played you on the organ, and you were too lovely to come out as a sound." He was simply stating what he believed.

She sat above him and turned her head. She gave him an unfathomable half-smile, and as she drew her breath the golden glow from behind her crept around her cheek and tinted the arched flesh of her nostrils. It was an exquisite gesture; she saw in his eyes that she had pleased him and thought, He stinks of grease and ammonia.

He put out his hand and touched her. He was actually afraid that she would slip back into a swelling of symphonic sound, sweep over him and be gone past all remembering.

"Are you a real woman who will be alive?" he faltered.

Stupid questions are not always stupid to stupid people. "Of course," she said.

Then he asked her to marry him.

She looked at his craggy face and boniness and his hollow chest and mad-looking eyes and shook her head. He backed away from her, turned and ran. He looked once over his shoulder, and caught the picture of her that lighted his brain until the day he died. For there, in light and shade, in warm flesh and cool colors, was the Largo; and he would have to live until he turned her back into music. He could not command her as she was; but if he could duplicate her in sharps and flats and heart-stopping syncopation, then she would be his. As he ran, staring back, his head thwacked on the doorpost, and he staggered on, all blood and tears.

Gretel looked pensively at her fingernails. "Good God," she said, "what a dope." And she went back to her cow-like mental vacancy.

A couple of nights later Gretel and Pascal Wylie were in a canoe on the hilltop lake, blandly violating the sacredness Drecksall had invested in her, when they heard music.

"What's that?" said Wylie sharply.

"Vi'lin," said Gretel. For her the subject closed with an almost audible snap, but Wylie's peering mind was diverted; and seeing this, she accepted it without protest, as she accepted all things. "Wonder who it is?" said Wylie. He touched a lever, and the silent solenoid-impulse motor in the stern of the canoe wafted them toward the sound.

"It's that kitchen-boy!" whispered Wylie a moment later.

Gretal roused herself enough to look. "He's crazy," she said coldly. She wished vaguely that Wylie would take her away from the sound of the violin, or that Drecksall would stop playing. Or—play something else. She had never heard these notes before, which was not surprising considering the kind of music Drecksall played. But such music had never bothered her until now. Very little ever bothered her. She made an almost recognizable effort to understand why she didn't like it, realized that it made her feel ashamed, assumed that she was ashamed because she was out with Wylie, and dropped the matter. Having reasoned past the music itself, she was no longer interested. She might have been had she realized that it was her own portrait in someone's else's eyes that she had listened to.

Wylie felt himself stirred too, but differently. It didn't matter to him why this scullery lad was scraping a fiddle on the lakeshore when he should have been asleep. The thing that struck him was that the man could make that violin talk. He made it get inside you—inside people who didn't give a damn, like Wylie. Wylie began to wonder why the hands that performed that way had taken on a duty of washing pots. He had learned early that the best way to get along (to him that meant to get rich) was to find your best talent and exploit it. Here was a man wasting a talent on trees and fish.

Music is a science as well as an art, and it is a shocking thing to those who think that musicians are by nature incompetent and impractical, to discover that more often than not a musician has a strong mechanical flair. Conversely, a person who is unmechanical is seldom musical. Drecksall's playing on this particular night was careful, thoughtful, precise. He was building something quite as tangible to him as a bridge is to an engineer. The future whole was awe-inspiring, beautiful, but, like the bridge, it was composed of quite unromantic essentials—tonal nuts, bolts and rivets. It was the skillfull machining of these that intrigued Wylie, possibly far more than would the completed work.

Drecksall paused at the end of a bewildering arpeggio, and stood with his violin in his hand, staring puzzledly across the water. He had just realized the enormity of his task, and was completely wrapped up in it, so was totally unprepared for Wylie's sudden burst of clapping. It was not applause, exactly; Wylie was gladhanding, following the birth of a bright idea. He had an idea he would butter up the violinist, befriend him, get him to someone who would know if he was really any good or not from a commercial point of view. If he was, Wylie could take a cut, maybe. Ten percent—forty—seventy-five? Drecksall was young. He would last a long time, and he looked like a dope.

So he cracked his lean hands together and whistled shrilly, like a grandfather at a burlesque house. Surely the ape would appreciate enthusiasm!

Drecksall leapt like a startled moose, nearly lost his footing, and then froze, peering toward the dark canoe, a hot smoke of anger curling into his brain. He felt stripped, imposed upon. He felt kicked. His night playing demanded infinitely more privacy than his body, and it was being rudely stared at. He suddenly broke the violin over his knee, hurled the pieces at the canoe, and ran into the dark woods.

"I told you he was crazy," said Gretel complacently.

It was a long time before Pascal Wylie could puff the wind back into his sails.

Two days later Drecksall was returning from a copse a hundred yards from the resort's main building, carrying a couple of large garbage pails. There was an incinerator back there, and as he left it he heard the whirring of rotary wings. He looked up and saw a cab descending, and would have ignored it altogether had he not noticed that the man who climbed out and paid the driver had a violin-case under his arm. Drecksall looked at it the way a prep-school boy looks at a soft-drink calendar.

"Hi," said Pascal Wylie. Drecksall nodded.

"I want to talk to you," said Wylie.

"Me?" Drecksall couldn't take his eyes off the violin.

"Yeh. Heard you lost your fiddle."

Drecksall just stared. Wylie grinned and handed over the instrument. Drecksall dropped his garbage cans, clasped the case and clawed it open. The violin was a good one, complete with three bows, spare strings, and a pitch pipe. Drecksall stood helplessly, his wide mouth trying fruitlessly to say the same thing his eyes were saying.

"You want that violin?" asked Wylie briskly. The question needed no answer. "It's yours if you'll do me a favor."

"What?"

Wylie gestured toward the cab. "Just hop in there with me. We'll run into the city, and you'll play that thing for a friend of mine. Chances are that after he hears you you can go right on playing as long as you want to, and you'll never wash another pot. How's it strike you?"

Drecksall looked at the tumbled garbage cans. "I can't leave here," he said. "I'd lose my job."

Wylie was not thinking about that. If the violinist failed the audition, he would starve—and he could, for all Wylie cared. But he thought the man had a chance. He snatched the violin and walked toward the cab. "Okay, then."

Drecksall picked up the cans and stared after Wylie. His would-be manager climbed in, giving not a backward glance. With elaborate carelessness, however, he did manage to have a great deal of difficulty in getting the violin-case in after him. It hung, black and shining and desirable, for seconds; and suddenly Drecksall realized just how badly those cans smelled. He ran to the cab and climbed in.

"Good boy," said Wylie.

Drecksall took the violin-case from him and opened it. "I never had a violin as nice as this before," he said simply.

The audition went off smoothly. Drecksall was led into a soundproof room containing a novachord and an unpleasing female organist. He was handed a sheaf of sheet music which, but for the individual titles, he thereafter ignored. A red light flashed, a speaker baffle said boredly, "Go ahead, please," and Drecksall played. He played for an hour, stopping twice in the middle of selections to tune his violin, which was new and springy, and once to upbraid the organist, who after the first few bars, had never played better in her life.

Afterward, in another room, Wylie was called in to speak to an official. He crossed the room and, with his hat on, perched easily on the edge of the man's desk and looked at his fingernails until the man spoke.

"You're this fellow's manager?"

"Mmm."

"Eight hundred for thirty minutes five times weekly, thirteen weeks." He dragged a contract form out of the desk, filled in some spaces, and shoved it over to Wylie. Wylie looked at it gingerly as if it was one of Drecksall's garbage pails, took the pen, crossed out the $800 and wrote in $5000. Then he yawned and looked out of the window.

"Don't be silly," said the radio executive. He looked keenly at Wylie, sighed, and drew up another contract. It was for two thousand. Wylie signed with alacrity. "Make that out in two checks, payable to cash," he said. "One eighteen hundred, and one two hundred."

The man behind the desk made out the checks. "Yours is the ten percent check?" he asked. Wylie smiled.

"I think you're a heel," said the exec, and handed the papers over.

At the door, Wylie tipped his hat and grinned. "Thank you very much, sir," he said. He went and found Drecksall and gave him his check. "Go buy yourself some clothes," he said. Drecksall looked at it and gasped.

"Two hundred dollars?"

Wylie nodded. "You're hired. Let's get out of here."

That was only the beginning. Wylie knew an amazing number of people, and before the year was out, Drecksall was nationally known. Money poured in, and, as Wylie was shrewd as well as slick, he saw to it that Drecksall got plenty. Since there was so much always on hand, Drecksall never questioned the cut that Wylie took, and Wylie was remarkably secretive about where he put his own money.

And one other thing of importance happened.

One afternoon Drecksall hurried home to the apartment he shared with Wylie in Safrisco. It was a quietly elaborate place, and it included the one thing Drecksall demanded—a totally soundproofed practice room. Flinging open the door, Drecksall was halfway across the sumptuous living room before he quite realized that on entering he had seen someone else in the room. He swung around, staring.

"Hello," said Gretel. She set down her drink and swung her feet off the couch. "Remember me?"

Drecksall nodded silently, watching her, stripping gloves off his hands.

"You're changed," he said after a bit, looking at her clothes, her hair.

"I should be." She smiled vapidly. "I'm married."

"Oh." It penetrated slowly. "Who to?"

"Pascal."

"He—he changed you?"

Gretel's bird-brain manufactured a bird's laugh. "Sure."

"Good God," whispered Drecksall in disgust. He went into his room and closed the door. He had just begun to hate Wylie.

Gretel picked up her drink again. "He's still crazy," she said.

In nearly all things Vernon Drecksall was as reasonably sane as the rest of us; but he was a monomaniac, and he could hardly be blamed for assuming the things he did. He and his odd conception of Gretel were made for each other. He was the form-fitting husk for his vision of her, and she had filled it completely. She could never do so again, because so much of that vision was composed of sunset gold and purple shadow and that unforgettable tinge of pink when the light shone through her nostril. He could not be expected to understand that. He only knew that the vision didn't fit any more; that something had happened to change her from that utter perfection. And he had her own word for it that Pascal Wylie was that thing. He slumped into the most driving kind of misery. He couldn't see that there was anything he could do about it except to go ahead with his building. Some day he would have her back. Some day she would emerge from his violin in a great bubble of melody which would settle before him, open up and reveal her there as she had been on that summer evening. And she would be his. Toward that iridescent ideal, he strove. Hour upon hour, alone in his soundproofed cell, he wrought the Largo. Sometimes he was rewarded by sustained flashes of completion. He had a phrase for her hair, a swift run for her strange eyes as she turned her head, a dazzling contrapuntal passage for the sound of her voice. Each little detail that was mastered was carefully scored, and he would play them jealously now and again, seeing his visions, spurring himself on to represent the duller notes which represented the more prosaic part of the picture—the windowframe behind her, the scratched surface of the old Hammond organ, the crack at the side of her shoe.

During the war, and the ruinous period afterward, he was glad that there was no longer any time for concerts or broadcasts or public appearances, for it left him time to work. Deep in the heart of a half-ruined hotel he labored by candlelight, while the three great counter-revolutions rolled and swirled around his little citadel of silence. Twice he saw Pascal Wylie in a gibbering state of fear; both times he had thrown him bodily out of his practice-room, ignoring his pleading and his warning that they were all going to be shot. Wylie was in politics up to his ears and over, though fortunately for him he had stayed in the background and let dollars speak for him. When it was all over and the exhausted world began to build again, Drecksall was possibly the only man alive who neither knew nor cared what had happened. He had been touched by it too; his investments were completely wiped out, but that meant nothing to him. He was certain that there would be more, and he was right. The Great Change was on, and with the nation's rebirth there was plenty for such as he.

And so the years swept by him as had the violence of war and revolution and renascence. Time left him alone, and it was with something of a shock that Wylie, during that rocky period, realized that the strange creature was the only solid, unchanging thing in the universe. Gretel changed by the day, for hers was the scintillant peasant beauty that fades early. She gave every promise of finally occupying some chimney-corner until she grew into a gargoyle and became part of the mantel. Wylie cared for her casually from force of habit, and bent his efforts to rebuilding his fortune. And Drecksall played.

Something else was creeping into the building of the Largo. The central theme itself, that breathing, mutant reproduction of Gretel, was being framed in a darker, deeper mass of tones. It was a thing like hatred, like vengeance, that frame. It was Pascal Wylie, and it wound round and about the thing that was Gretel. This was not mere music. This was something more definite than even Drecksall's crazed kind of music. It was the outline, the detailed description, of a definite plan of action. The same impulse that drove him to do something about his vanished Gretel was forcing him to deal, in his own way, with Wylie.

There came a time when Drecksall felt that the Largo was nearly complete. It would need more than scoring for the composition to be fully rounded. It would need an audience, and it would need a setting. It couldn't be played in any ordinary concert hall, nor in the open air. For its full effect, it must needs be played in an auditorium built for it, and it alone.

A building like that never existed, nor did Drecksall expect it to. He built it himself. It took two years or more. It cost thousands—so much, indeed, that he went to Wylie for more; and Wylie, fearing that he would begin asking questions, gave him more and more of his own earnings, telling him blandly that theater managers and the broadcasting chains were paying more these days. Drecksall didn't care, as long as he got enough for his purpose.

He had no end of trouble. It was months before he found an engineer who would dare attempt the auditorium, more months before he found one who could be convinced that he meant what he said when he gave his specifications. They were to be followed to the thousandth of a millimeter, and Drecksall's rages when he saw tiny variations on the blueprints were really beautiful to behold. In time, the indignant word, "After all, Mr. Drecksall, I'm a graduate engineer, and while you may be the world's foremost violinist, you are not qualified to—" became real poison to him. After breaking up a few expensive violins and accessories over their erudite heads, he gave up personal visits from architects and contractors and handled the thing vitriolically, by mail.

But when the auditorium was finished, it was what he had ordered, from the bedrock and soil he had specified to the top of the heavy square tower. It was certainly a strange affair. It was not very large, and looked like the conventionalized nose of a space cruiser. Its walls were thin at the bottom, thick and massive at its domed top. Inside the basic construction was easily seen. It was made of thirty-eight arches all joining at the top and forming the circular walls at the sides and base. The tower was squat and massive; solid, steel-reinforced concrete. There were no windows, and the door was self-sealing, an integral part of its wall. It was lighted from a fixture which also was built into the contours of the wall. The only thing that detracted from that symphony of metrical lines on the interior wall was a heavy concrete block that jutted out over a stone chair—high over it. On the other side of the chamber was another such chair, but the wall over it was like all the others. At the exact center of the building was a tiny red tile, set into the floor, and this was the only indication of a stage, a place from which to perform. It was certainly a strange creation; but then, it had been built for a strange purpose.

Drecksall made his demands several weeks before he intended to play the Largo, because he expected resistance. He got it. Wylie failed to see why he should sit through a highly involved musical masterpiece when he had never cared particularly for music; why he should go out into the wild, miles from the nearest city, to hear it; why it couldn't be played in the apartment or at their country place; and most particularly, why he should rouse Gretel from the intellectual stupor she had fallen into these last years and drag her out there to the auditorium. Drecksall heard him out patiently, said, "It really isn't much to ask," and left the room. He was back in a moment with the concert violin which he wrapped carefully in a plexiskin and put away in its case. "I'm not going to play again," he said quietly, "until I play the Largo for you and Gretel, in my auditorium." Then, leaving Wylie to give puzzled shrugs at the violin-case, he went out.

It took just forty-eight hours for Wylie to discover that Drecksall was really serious, for it was that long before the violinist had an engagement. Wylie got into his soup and fish, went to call Drecksall, and found him sprawled smiling on the couch of his practice room. He refused to go. Fuming, Wylie canceled the concert. He didn't give in on that occasion, nor on the next, but when he read a note on one of the fasci-papers to the effect that the Old Master was at long last developing temperament, and that perhaps the word "maybe" should be inserted before the date of each of his scheduled concerts, Wylie broke down, at last asking himself why he had made an issue of it at all. Drecksall had been easy enough to get along with.

And at long last they hired a heliplane and whirred the long miles out to the auditorium. As they landed, Wylie broke his glum silence to ask, "How long'll we be here?"

"I couldn't say," grinned Drecksall happily.

"How long will it take to play the thing?"

"About an hour."

"Shall I tell him to come back in about that time?" asked Wylie, nodding toward the cab-driver.

Drecksall alighted from the cab and helped Gretel out. "If you like," he said.

The plane shot away and they walked up the rough trail toward the auditorium. "That the place?" asked Wylie.

"That's the place."

Wylie looked at it. "Hell! What did you go and spend all that jack on that place for? Why, it wouldn't hold fifty people!"

"It wasn't meant to," said Drecksall gently.

They reached the door—that is, the point where the path ended against the wall. Drecksall paused and looked at them.

"You have a hard collar on," he said. "Take it off."

"Take—what for?"

"This building is the last word—*my* last word—in

acoustics. I can't have anything spoiling it." He looked at Gretel. She was standing there, uncomplaining as ever. "Tell her to take off those stockings, too. They're sheet plastic, and might echo."

Wylie glanced over his shoulder at the speck that was the retreating heliplane, shrugged, and took off his collar. "Take your stockings off," he said to Gretel.

The spasm that signified mental activity crossed Gretel's bland face. "He's crazy," she said, looking at Drecksall.

"You're kiddin'," said Wylie. "Go on—take 'em off."

Once that was disposed of, Drecksall opened the door and followed them in. He turned on the lights, closed the door. "Sit over there," he said to Wylie, indicating the stone seat under the jutting block. He led Gretel over to the other chair. Then he took his violin out and put the case into a recess in the wall. A panel slid over it.

"This is a looney sort of place," said Wylie. His voice echoed so that it hurt his ears. For his own comfort, he whispered. "What gave you the idea for it?"

Drecksall stopped rubbing his bow with rosin to stare at his manager. "What gave me the idea? Study, you fool. Years of it. Infinite patience in going into the laws and phenomena and—and tricks of acoustics. Be quiet. I'm going to play."

He snuggled the tail of the violin into the hollow of his throat, bowed the open strings, flattened one of them microscopically. Then, without another word, he began to play.

Little else could be said here than that he played his Largo. It began stridently, weaving that dreadful flaming frame for the vision of Gretel; and Wylie was whisked deep into it. One part of his brain ticked busily away, still wondering about this auditorium, the fact that it was built for an audience of two, the surprise in discovering that for years Drecksall had had a secret activity, the realization that the acoustics of the place were indeed amazing. The notes spread out from his inspired violin, were gathered at the top of the dome and hurled back with a force that made the building tremble. Yes, the building echoed; soon, it had far more echoed sound in it than original, so that Drecksall could slip into a thin, sweet piping and be accompanied by a tumultuous background of sound that he had created long seconds before.

The music suddenly took an ear-shattering turn, and then began a theme—a theme that caught both Wylie and the comatose Gretel the same way, made them both stretch their memories back and back until they settled on a dark lake. They saw again a figure on a rock, pressing notes out through the warm air on a hilltop lake. The same theme—and then again that crashing series of bass runs; and then, before the listeners had time to be startled by it, that almost tele-pathic theme again. Back and back again he returned to it, the roar of the base strings and the compelling measures of the memory theme; and always they were faster, and louder, and closer together. They blended finally into a great crescendo, a monster welling of sound that gathered in the dome and came crashing down, pressing the stone block away from the wall, sending its massive tons down on Pascal Wylie. Its crash was symphonic precisely blended with the mood and rhythm of the music; and as the echoes died away, that whole section of floor sank out of sight, bearing Wylie's crushed body and the pile of rubble that hid it; and a panel slid across the opening. Now the auditorium was acoustically perfect for the greater task that was at hand.

Gretel sat in a paralysis of fear, and Drecksall played earnestly on. This part of the Largo was justice. He had long wanted to kill Wylie because Wylie, he felt, had killed the Gretel he pictured. But artistic integrity forbade the use of any weapon but music, for music was so deeply involved.

And now began the recreation of his old, old vision. He did not look at the unmoving Gretel, but sketched in the essentials of his tone-portrait, and then went over them and over them, filling in. He never lost sight of the shades he had already drawn, but all the while he strove for more and more perfect completion. Even Gretel began to see it. The music moved, with mechanical perfection, across her mental screen, burning indelibly wherever it touched. It moved with speed, slowly, the way the darting photoelectric beam slowly draws a transmitted photograph. It moved as indirectly and as purposefully and as implacably.

The laboring strings hummed and crackled, and Drecksall's fingers were a blur. Gretel, shockingly, felt the fabric of the clothes she had worn that day, all over her body; she felt the warmth of the setting sun on her back, and her lips began to move in the words she had spoken then, so vivid was the music.

And then, shrilly, the thing was complete. The picture was there sustained by one thin, high note that fell and fell until it became low and vibrant and infinitely compelling. It continued unbearably, filling the room, filling it again at twice the pressure, again and again. A trickle of powdered stone came down from the tower's base, and then the tortured stone could stand no more. The upper walls cracked and the tower burst through.

And as it did, Vernon Drecksall saw and claimed his reward. The mass of masonry opened high over his head and a shaft of golden sunlight speared through, and in the roaring, dust-filled auditorium Gretel sat spotlighted. Her pose, her hair, her very expression, were, to his crazed and triumphant mind, the Largo, come alive. With a glad cry he hurled his violin away and caught her in his arms on the very instant that the great tower crushed down on them both. He had his revenge, and he had his consummation.

The chandeliers on the eighty-first floor of the Empire State Building swung wildly without any reason. A company of soldiers marched over a new, well-built bridge, and it collapsed. Enrico Caruso filled his lungs and sang, and the crystal glass before him shattered.

And Vernon Drecksall composed his Largo.

THE BONES

Donzey came to the door with a pair of side-cutting pliers in his hand and soldering flux smeared on the side of his jaw. "Oh—Farrel. Come in."

"Hi, Donzey." The town's police force ducked his head under the doorway and followed the mechanic through a littered living room into what had once been a pantry. It was set up as a workshop, complete with vises, a power lathe, a small drill press and row upon row of tools. It was a great deal neater than the living room. By the window was a small table on which was built an extraordinarily complicated radio set which featured a spherical antenna and more tubes and transformers and condensers than a small-town bicycle repairman can be expected to buy and still eat. Farrel added a stick of gum to his already over-size wad and stared at it.

"That it?" he asked.

"That's it," said Donzey proudly. He sat down beside the table and picked up an electric soldering iron. "She ought to work this time," he said, holding the iron close to his cheek to see if it were hot enough.

"And I used to think FM was the initials of a college," said Farrel.

"Not in radio," said Donzey. The lump of solder in his hand slumped into glittering fluidity, sealed a joint. "And this is a different kind of frequency modulation, too. This is the set that's going to make us some real money, Farrel."

"Yeah," said the sheriff without enthusiasm. He was thinking of the irrepressible Donzey's flotation motor, that was supposed to use the power developed by a chain of hollow balls floating to the top of a tank; of his ingenious plan for zoning highways by disappearing concrete walls between the lanes—a swell idea only somebody else had patented it. Also there was a little matter of a gun which could be set to fire thirty bullets at any interval between a fifth of a second to thirty minutes. Only nobody wanted it. Donzey was as unsuccessful as he was enthusiastic. He kept body and soul indifferently together only because he had infinite powers of persuasion. He could sell one of his ideas to the proverbial brass monkey—more; he could get a man like Farrel to invest capital in an idea like his directional FM transmitter. His basic principle was a signal beamed straight up, which would strike the heaviside layer and bounce *almost* straight down, thus being receivable only in the receiver at which it was aimed. Donzey had got the idea over at the pool parlor. If you could aim an eight-ball at a six-ball, off the cushion, you ought to be able to aim a signal from the transmitter to the receiver, off the heaviside layer. The thing would be handy as a wireless field telephone for military liaison.

Of course, Donzey knew little about radio. But he always worked on the theory that logic was as good or better than book-learning. His mind was as incredibly facile as his stubby fingers. What it lacked in exactitude it made up for in brilliance. Seeing the wiring on the set, an electrical engineer would have sighed and asked Donzey if he was going to put tomato sauce on all that spaghetti. Donzey would have called the engineer a hidebound conservative. Because of Donzey's pragmatic way of working, the world will never know the wiring diagram of that set. Donzey figured that if it worked he could build more like it. If it didn't, who cared how it was made?

Donzey laid the soldering iron on the bed it had charred out for itself on the workbench, brushed back his wiry black hair without effect, and announced that he was ready. "She may not work just yet," he said, plugging the set in and holding his breath for a moment in silent prayer until he was sure that the fuse was not going to blow. "But then again she might." When the tubes began to glow, he cut in the loud-speaker. It uttered a horrifying roar; he tuned it down to a hypnotic hum.

Farrel folded himself into a chair and stared glumly at the proceedings, wondering whether or not he would ever get his twenty-eight dollars and sixty cents out of this contraption. Donzey switched off the speaker and handed him a headset. "Put these on and see what you get."

Farrel clamped the phones over his ears and tried to look bored. Donzey went back to his knobs and dials.

"Anything yet?"

"Yeah." Farrel shifted his cud. "It howls like a houn' dawg."

Donzey grunted and put a finger on one phone connection and a thumb on the other. Farrel swore and snatched off the headset. "What you tryin' to do," he growled, rubbing a large, transparent ear, "make me deef?"

"Easy with the phones, son." Donzey was fifteen years younger than the sheriff, but he could say "son" and make it stick. "Phone condenser's shot. And that's the last .00035 I have. Got to rig up something. Wait a minute." He flew out of the room.

Farrel sighed and walked over to the window. Donzey was locally famous for the way he "rigged things up." He rigged up a supercharger for the municipal bandit-chaser which really worked, once you got used to its going backward in second gear. Farrell was not at all surprised to see Donzey out in the yard, busily rummaging through the garbage can.

He entered the room a moment later, unabashedly blowing the marrow out of a section of mutton bone. "Got a cigarette?" he said, wiping his mouth. Farrel dourly handed over a pack. Donzey ripped it open, spilling the smokes over the workbench. He stripped off the tinfoil, tore it in half, and after cleaning up the bone inside and out with Farrel's handkerchief, poked some of the foil into the bone and wrapped it carefully in the other piece. "Presto," he said. "A condenser."

"My handkerchief—" began Farrel.

"You'll be able to buy yourself a trainload of 'em when we put this on the market," said Donzey with superb confidence. He busily connected the outside layer of tinfoil to one phone plug and the inside wad to the other. "Now," he said, handing the earphones to the sheriff, "that ought to do it. I'm sending from this key. There's no connection between transmitter and receiver. The signal's going straight up—I hope. It should come straight down."

"But I don't know that dit-dot stuff," said Farrel, putting on the headset nevertheless.

"Don't have to," said Donzey. "I'll play *Turkey in the Straw*. You ought to recognize that."

They sat down and again Donzey switched on the juice. His fingers found the key as his eyes found Farrel's face; and then his fingers forgot about the key.

Farrel's heavy lids closed for a long second, while his lantern jaw slowly lit up. Then the eyes began to open, slowly. At just the halfway mark, they stopped and the man did something extraordinary with his nostrils. A long sigh escaped him, and his wide lips flapped resoundingly in the breeze. His head tilted slowly to one side.

"Mmmwaw," he said.

"Farrel!" snapped Donzey, horrified.

"M-m-ba-a-a—"

Before Donzey could reach him he reared up out of his chair, tossing his head back. By some miracle the earphones stayed in place. Farrel's hands hit the floor; he landed on one palm and one wrist, which grated audibly. His huge feet kicked out and his arms gave way. He landed on his face, the wire from the headset tightened and the table on which the radio stood began to lean out from the wall. Donzey squalled and put out his arms to catch his darling; and catch it he did. His hands gripped the chassis, perfectly grounded, and as he hugged the set to him to save it, the upper terminal of a 6D6 tube contacted his chin. He suddenly felt as if a French 75 had gone off in his face. He saw several very pretty colors. One of them, he recalled later, looked like the smell of a rose, and another looked like a loud noise. He hit the floor with a bump, numbed instinct acting just far enough to twist his body under the precious radio. Nothing broke but the power line; and as soon as that parted, Farrel scrambled most profanely to his feet.

"Get up, you hind-end of a foot," he roared, "so I can slap you down again!"

"Wh-wh-whoooee!" said Donzey's lungs, trying to get the knack of breathing again.

"Go away," breathed the quivering mass under the radio. Donzey waited a few seconds, and when Farrel still continued to hang over him, he decided to go on waiting. He knew that the canny old sheriff would never plow through a cash investment to get to him. As long as the radio was perched on his chest he was safe.

"Who you fink you're pwayin' twickf on?" said the sheriff through a rapidly swelling lip.

"I wasn't pwaying any twickf," mimicked Donzey. "Sizzle down, bud. What happened?"

"I ftarted to go cwavy, vat's all. What kind of devil'f gadget iv vat anyway?"

Sensing that the sheriff's anger was giving way to self-pity, Donzey took a chance on lifting the radio off himself. "My gosh, man—you're hurt!"

Farrel followed Donzey's eyes to his rapidly swelling wrist. "Yeah . . . I— Hey! It hurts!" he said, surprised.

"It should," said Donzey. While Farrel grunted, he bound it against a piece of board, and then went for a couple of ice cubes for the now balloon-like lip. As soon as Farrel was comfortable, Donzey started asking questions.

"What happened when I switched on the set?"

Farrel shuddered. "It was awful. I seen pictures."

"Pictures? You mean—pictures, like television?"

Donzey's gadgeteer's heart leaped at the ideas that thronged into his cluttered mind. Maybe his set, by some odd circuiting, could induce broadcast television signals directly on the mind! Maybe he had invented an instrument for facilitating telepathy. Mayhe he had stumbled on something altogether new and unheard of. Any way you looked at it, there was millions in it. *Piker,* he told himself, *there's billions in it!*

"Nah," said Farrel. His face blanched; like many a bovine character before him he suddenly realized he had swallowed his cud.

"Don't worry about it," said the observant Donzey. "Chewing gum won't hurt you. Chew some more and forget it. Now, about those pictures—"

"Them . . . they wasn't like television. They wasn't like nothin' I ever heard about before. They were colored pictures—"

"Moving pictures?"

"Oh, yeah. But they were all foggy. Things close to me, they were clear. Anything more'n thirty feet away was—fuzzy."

"Like a camera out of focus?"

"Um. But things 'way far away, they were clear as a bell."

"What did you see?"

"Hills—fields. I didn't recognize that part of the country. But it all looked different. The grass was green, but sort of gray, too. An' the sky was just—blank. It all seemed good. I dunno—you won't laugh at me, Donzey?" asked the sheriff suddenly.

"Good gosh no!"

"Well, I was—*eatin'* the grass!" Farrell peered timidly at the mechanic and then seemed reassured. "It was queer. I couldn't figure time at all. I don't know how long it went on—might 'a' been years. Seemed like it was raining sometimes. Sometimes it was cold, an' that didn't bother me. Sometimes it was hot, and boy, that did."

"Are you telling me you *felt* things in those pictures?"

Farrel nodded soberly. "Donzey, I was *in* those pictures."

Donzey thought, *What have I got here? Transmigration? Teleportation? Clairvoyance? Why, there's ten billion in it!*

"What got me," said Farrel thoughtfully, "was that everything seemed so good. Until the end. There was miles of alleys, like, and then a great big dark building. I was scared, but everyone else seemed to be going my way, so I went along. Then some feller with a . . . a cleaver, he . . . I tried to get away, but I couldn't. He hit me. I hollered."

"I'll say you did." They shuddered together for a moment.

"That's all," said Farrel. "He hit me twice, and I woke up on the floor with a busted wing and saw you all mixed up with the radio. Now you tell me—what happened?"

"You seemed to go into a kind of trance. You hollered, and then started thrashing around. You did a high-dive onto the deck an' dragged the radio off the table. I caught it an' my chin hit it when it was hot. It knocked me silly. The whole thing didn't last twenty seconds."

"Donzey," said the sheriff, standing up, "you can keep the money I put into this thing. I don't want no more of it." He went to the door. "Course, if you should make a little money, don't forget who helped you get a start."

Donzey laughed. "I'll keep in touch with you," he said. "Look—about that big building you went into You said you were scared, but everybody else was going the same way, so you went along. What were the others like?"

Farrel looked at him searchingly. "Did I say 'everybody else'?"

"You did."

"That's funny." Farrell scratched his head with his unbandaged arm. "All the rest of 'em was—sheep." And he went out.

For a long time after Farrel had gone, Donzey sat and stared at the radio. "Sheep," he muttered. He got up and set the transmitter carefully back on the table, rapidly checking over the wiring and tubes to see that all was safe and unbroken. "Sheep?" he asked himself. What had an FM radio to do with sheep? He put away his pliers and sal ammoniac and solder and flux; hung his friction tape on its peg; picked up the soldering iron by the point and was reminded that it was still plugged in. He looked down at his scorched palm. "Sheep!" he said absently.

It wasn't anything you could just figure out, like what made an automobile engine squeak when you ran it more than two hundred miles without any oil, or why most of the lift comes from the top surface of an airplane's wing. It was something you had to try out, like getting drunk or falling in love. Donzey switched on the radio, sat down and picked up the headset. As he adjusted the crownpiece back down to man-size, he was struck by an ugly thought. Farrel had been in a bad way when he was inside this headset. He was—dreaming, was it?—that some guy was striking him with a cleaver just as she lurched forward and cut the juice. Suppose he hadn't cut it—would he have died, like the . . . the sheep he thought he was?

Donzey lay the earphones down and went into the bedroom for his alarm clock. Bolting it to the table, he wrapped a cord around the alarm key and led it to the radio switch. Then he set it carefully, so that it would go off in one minute and turn off the set. He put on the headset, waited twenty-five seconds, and turned it on. Fifteen seconds to warm up, and then—

It happened for him, too, that gray grass and blank sky, the timelessness, the rain, the cold, the heat, and the sheep. The—*other* sheep. He ate the grass and it was good. He was frightened and milled with the others through those alleyways. He saw the dark building. He—and the alarm shrilled, the set clicked off, and he sat there sweating, a-tremble. This was bad. Oh, but bad.

And money in it? Would anybody pay for pictures you could live in? And die in?

He had a wholesome urge to take his little humdinger—a machinist's hammer—and ding the hum out of the set. He got the better of the urge. He did, however, solemnly swear never to eat another bite of lamb or mutton. That noise Farrel had made—

Mutton? Wasn't there some mutton involved in the radio? He looked at it—at the phone condenser. An innocent-looking little piece of bone, hollow, with the tinfoil inside and out. Giggling without mirth, he took a piece of wire and shorted the homemade condenser out of the circuit, set his time switch, and put on the phones. Nothing happened. He reached over, snatched the wire away. Immediately he was eating gray-green grass under a blank sky, and it was good—

good—and now the cold and then the alarm, and he was back in his chair, staring at the muttonbone condenser.

"That bone," he whispered, "just ain't dead yet!"

He went and stood at the front door, thinking of the unutterable horror of that dark building, the milling sheep. Farrel's sprained wrist. The mutton bone. "Somewhere, somehow," he told himself, "there's a hundred billion in it!"

Ringing a doorbell with a hand burdened by a huge bundle of groceries while the other is in a sling, presents difficulties, but Sheriff Farrel managed it. Turning the knob was harder, but Farrel managed that, too, when there was no response to the bell. From the inside room came the most appalling series of sounds—a chuckling, hysterical gabbling which rose in pitch until it was cut off with a frightful gurgling. Farrel tossed his burden on a seedy divan and ran into the workshop.

Donzey was lolling in the chair by the radio with the earphones on. His face was pale and his eyes were closed, and he twitched. The radio, in the two weeks since Farrel had seen it, had undergone considerable change. It was now compactly boxed in a black enameled sheet-iron box, from which protruded the controls and a pair of adjustable steel clips, which held what looked like a small white stick. The old speaker, the globular antenna, and all of the external spaghetti was gone. Among the dials on the control panel was that of a clock with a sweep second-hand. This and Donzey's twitching were the only movements in the room.

Suddenly the set clicked and Donzey went limp. Farrel gazed with sad apprehension at the mechanic, thinking that being his pallbearer would be little trouble.

"Donzey—"

Donzey shook his head and sat up. He was thinner, and his eyes told the sheriff that he was in the throes of something or other. He leaped up and pumped Farrel's good hand. "Just the man I wanted to see. It works, Farrel—it works!"

"Yeah, we're rich," said Farrel dourly. "I heard all that before. Heck with it. Come out o' here." He dragged Donzey into the living room and indicated the bundle on the divan. "Start in on that."

Donzey investigated. "What's this for?"

"Eatin', dope. The whole town's talkin' about you starvin' yourself. If I hadn't given you that money, you wouldn't have built that radio."

"Well, you don't have to feed me," said Donzey warmly.

"I feed any stray dog that follers me home," said Farrel. "An' I ain't responsible for 'em bein' hungry. Eat, now."

"Who said I was hungry?"

"Goes without sayin'. A guy that goes scrabblin' around Tookey's butcher shop lookin' for bones twice a day just ain't gettin' enough Vitamin B."

Donzey laughed richly, looked at the sheriff and laughed again. "Oh—that! I wasn't hungry!"

"Don't start pullin' the wool over my eyes. You'll eat that stuff or I'll spread it on the floor an' roll you in it." He took the bag and upended it over the couch.

Donzey, with awe, looked at the bread, the butter, the preserves, canned fruit, steak, potatoes, lard, vegetables—"Farrel, for gosh sakes! Black market. It must be, for all that—"

"It ain't," said the sheriff grimly. He herded Donzey into the kitchen, brushed a lead-crucible and a miniature steam engine off the stove, and started to cook.

Donzey protested volubly until the steak started to sizzle and then was stopped by an excess of salivary fluid. He was a little hungry, after all.

Farrel kept packing it in him until he couldn't move, and then sat down opposite and began to eye him coldly. "Now what's all this about?" he asked. "Why didn't you come to me for a handout?"

"I didn't need a handout," said Donzey, "and if I did I was too busy to notice it. Farrel, we've got the biggest thing of the century sitting in there!"

"It shoots a signal where you want it to, like you said?"

"Huh? What do you . . . Oh, you mean the heaviside-beam thing? Nah," said Donzey with scorn. "Son, this is *big*!"

"Hm-m-m," said Farrel, looking at his sling. "But what good is it?"

"An entirely new school of thought will be built up around this thing," exulted Donzey. "It touches on philosophy, my boy, and metaphysics—the psychic sciences, even."

"What good is it?"

"Course, I can only guess on the whys and wherefores. When you came in, I was a chicken. I got my neck wrung. Sound silly? Well, it wouldn't to you . . . you *know*. But nobody else would believe me. I was a chicken—"

"What good is it?"

"—because between the clips I've built on the set I put a sliver of chicken bone. There was mutton on it when you tried it. I've been cattle and swine through that gadget, Farrel. I've been a sparrow and a bullfrog and an alley cat and a rock bass. I know how each one of them lived and died!"

"Swell," said Farrel. "But what good is it?"

"What good is it? How can you ask me such a question? Can't you think of anything but money?"

This sudden reversal caught Farrel right between the eyes. He rose with dignity, as if he were sitting on an elevator. "Donzey," he said, "you're a thief an' a robber, an' I don't want no more to do with you. Miz' Curtis was sayin' the other day that Donzey is a boy that's goin' places. I guess it's up to me to tell you where to go." He told him and stamped out.

Donzey laughed, reached for a toothpick and set about enjoying the last of that delicious steak. Farrel was a nice guy, but he lacked imagination.

Come to think of it, what good *was* the gadget?

Two hours later a small package was delivered. It contained a note and a splinter of bone. The note read:

I know I'm bein a fool, but I can't forget the first time I met that FM thing of yours. Maybe for once in your life you can put one of your contraptions to work.

Seems as how Billy Kelley just was in here wantin me to trace his wife Eula. They been havin fights—well, you know Bill, he always treated her like she was in third grade. I often wondered why she didn't take out a long time ago, the way he used to smack her around and all, and seems like she did.

Bill allows she has run out with somebody, he don't know who. Anyway, right after he left a deputy comes in and says he has found Eula out on the highway in her car. Says she is all busted up. I drove out there and sure enough there she is. She is all by herself and she is dead. Car climbed a power pole on the wrong side of a cyclone fence. What I want you to find out is whether there was anyone with her. She had a compound fracture and it wasn't no trouble to get this sample. See what you can get.

FARREL.

Donzey realized that he still had the bone splinter in his hand. He laid it quickly on the table and stared at it as if he expected it to moan at him. He had known for some time that he would have to get a human bone to experiment with, but he would rather have had an anonymous one. He had known Eula Kelley for years. Farrel's clumsy note didn't begin to state the tragedy of her life since she married the town's rich man. She was a Kelley, and she had been a Walsh before that, and he wasn't surprised that she had finally decided to leave him. But it didn't make sense that she had left with another man. Not Eula.

Feeling a little sick, Donzey clipped the bone into his machine, set it for twenty seconds, put on the phones and threw the switch. He sat quite still until it clicked off, and then, white and shaken, adjusted the time switch for forty seconds. Once again he "listened," then made his final setting of fifty-two seconds—enough to take him right up to the mental image of Eula's death. More than that he dared not do. His great fear was that some day his psychic identification with the bone's individuality would be carried with it into death.

Farrel arrived and found him sitting on the steps, his jaw muscles knotting furiously, his sharp eyes full of puzzled anger. Farrel left a deputy in his car and went inside with Donzey.

"Get anything?" he asked.

"Plenty. Farrel, that Billy Kelley ought to be shot, and I'd like to do the shooting."

"Yeah. He's a louse. That ain't our affair. Was there anyone with her?"

"I—think there was. You better see for yourself."

Farrel shot him a quizzical glance and then sat down beside the machine. Donzey turned it on as the sheriff donned the headset, and then sat back, watching. He was sorry that he had to put Farrel through it, but he felt that the sheriff should know the story that splinter had to tell. His mind ran back over Eula's idea-patterns, the images they yielded. It was a story of incredible sordidness, and of a man's utter cruelty to a woman. It told of the things he had done, things he had said. Eula had borne it and borne it, and her ego had slowly been crushed under the weight of it. Then there was that last terrible incident, and she had run away from him. It didn't matter where she was running to, as long as it was away. And there was the flight of hope, the complete death of relief, when she realized, out there on the highway, that there was no escape. Bill Kelley's mark was on her; she couldn't leave him or her life with him. She knew exactly what she was doing when she threw the wheel hard over and closed her eyes against the beginnings of that tearing crash.

* * *

The set clicked off. Farrel stared at Donzey, and drew a deep, shuddering breath.

"It don't seem right Donzey, knowing things like that about a woman. I always knew Bill was a snake, but—"

"Yeah," said Donzey. "I know."

Farrel peeled off the headset and went to the door. "Harry," he called to his deputy, "go get Bill Kelley."

"What's that for?" asked Donzey when he returned.

"Strictly outside the law," said Farrel very quietly, "I'm goin' to give Bill Kelley somethin' he needs." He took off his badge and laid it on the bench.

Donzey suddenly remembered hearing that, years ago, Eula Walsh had married Bill Kelley when she was engaged to Farrel. He wondered if he would have called Farrel in if he had remembered that before, and decided that he would have.

"Farrel," he said after a time, "about that other person in the car—"

Farrel's big head came up. "That's right—there was somebody—I got just the impression of it, just before the crash. I don't rightly remember—seems like it was someone I know, though."

"Me, too. I can't understand it, Farrel. She wasn't running away with anybody. She wasn't interested in anybody or anything except in getting away. I didn't get any intimation of her meeting anyone, or even being with anyone until that last few seconds."

"That's right. What did he look like?"

"Sort of . . . well, medium sized and . . . damn if I remember. But I don't think I've seen him before."

"I haven't, either," said Donzey. "I don't know that it's really important. If she ran away with somebody, she rated it. I don't think she did, but . . . heck, he was probably just a hitchhiker that she was too upset to think about," he finished lamely.

"A woman don't commit suicide with a stranger along," Farrel said.

"A woman's liable to do anything after she's been through what Eula went through." The doorbell pealed. "That'll be Kelley."

As Farrel went to the door, Donzey noticed that his palms were wet. Farrel opened the door and the deputy's voice drifted in: "I saw Kelley, sheriff. He wouldn't come."

"He wouldn't come? Why?"

Harry's voice was aggrieved. "Aw, he seemed to have a wild hair up his nose. Got real mad. Started foamin' at the mouth. Said by golly the police were public servants. Said he wasn't used to bein' ordered around like a criminal. Said if you want to see him you got to come to him, or prove he committed a crime. Sour-castic son-of-a-gun."

"That ain't all he is," said Farrel. "Forget it, Harry. Shove off. I'll walk into town when I'm through here." He banged the door. "Donzey, we're goin' to fix that feller."

Donzey didn't like to see a big, easy-going lug like Farrel wearing that icy grin. The huge hands that pinned the badge back in its place shook ever so little.

"Sure," said Donzey futilely, "sure—we'll get him."

Farrel spun on his heel as if Kelly's face were under it, and stalked out.

It was about three days later that one of Farrel's stooges at the county hospital sent up a bone specimen from an appendictis death. Attached was a brief case history:

Cause of death, appendicitis. Age, about forty; male. Appendix ruptured suddenly in Sessions Restaurant at 8:30 p.m. Went on operating table about 9:15. Doctor in charge administered adrenalin by pericardial hypodermic. Patient roused sufficiently to allow operation. Removal of appendix and sponging of peritoneum successful. Death by post-operative hemorrhage, 9:28.

"We have," muttered Donzey as he clipped the bone into the machine, "a little scientist in our midst. Ol' Doc Grinniver up to his tricks again! A ruptured appendix and he tosses in a jolt of adrenalin to 'rouse' the patient, in the meantime making his heart pump poison all over his body, high-pressure." He picked up his earphones and glanced at the report again. " 'Post-operative hemorrhage' my blue eyeballs! That was peritonitis! Oh, well, I guess he would have died anyway, and I guess the old butcher couldn't get hold of a guinea pig with appendicitis." He sat down at the machine, adjusted the time switch, and his mind slipped into the bone emanations.

It was the usual life-and-death story, but with a difference. The man had been in the midst of a slimy little office intrigue which seemed to have taken command of most of his thoughts in the last few months; but the ragged stab of pain when his appendix burst drove all that out. Pain is like that, and Donzey had found that people handled it in two ways. They let it pile up on them until it suffocated them, or they floated up and up in it until it supported them; they lay in it like a bed. The second way, though, required a knack which took years to develop, and Donzey was glad he could learn it from other people's experience.

This particular case took it the first way, and it wasn't very nice. The agony grew and dimmed all his senses except the one that feels pain; and that grew. Pretty soon he couldn't even think. But when it got past that stage, it began to overwhelm his sensories, too, and the pain lessened. His eyes were open—had been, because he realized that his eyeballs were dry—but he slowly began to see again. Someone was bending over him. He was on the operating table. He had been to the movies, and he never remembered seeing anyone in dark clothes around an operating table before. And as his vision strengthened and the figure became clearer and clearer, he felt first curiosity, then awe, then the absolute, outside utmost in terror. Like a beam of negative energy, he felt it soaking up the heat of his body, his very life. It was a huge and monstrous thing. He had strength for just one thing; he closed his eyes just a tenth of a second before the dark one's face swam into focus; and then, in the same instant, the doctor's needle entered his heart. The warmth flowed back weakly, and when he dared to open his eyes again the dark one was gone.

And then the operation; and he felt every scrape and slice of it. When Donzey thought about it afterward he felt his own appendix literally squirm in sympathy—not an experience measuring up to the highest standards of animal comfort. Soon enough it was over, and the set clicked off with a nice life margin of two minutes to go.

Donzey sat for a long time thinking this over. His was a mechanic's mind, and such a mind seldom rejects anything because it has never heard of it before, or because it has heard otherwise. This machine now—it proposed certain very important questions.

Donzey spread the questions out on a blank spot in his brain and looked at them.

The machine showed what Death felt like, just before it happened. That was the really valuable point— it *happened*. it wasn't a light going out. It was a force swinging into action, so strong that it could impress itself on the carefully constructed thought-patterns mysteriously apparent in bones. All right—

What was this force called Death?

Donzey thought of that dark figure in the operating theater of the county hospital, and knew without a doubt that that question was answered. He was very happy that the late possessor of that piece of bone had had the consideration to close his eyes before he had taken a good look. Or was it the adrenalin that drove the dark thing out of sight? What had being in sight to do with death? Did looking on the Dark One—the capitalization was Donzey's—result in death? Could that be it? Were sickness and accidents merely phenomena that gave man the power to see death? And was that sight the thing that took their life force out of their now useless bodies? And—

Would seeing Death in the machine kill a man?

Donzey looked respectfully at the machine and thought, "I could easy enough try it and find out," without making the slightest move to do so.

Farrel arrived that evening, and for once the grim old man looked benignly happy. He clapped Donzey on the back, smiled, and sat down wordlessly.

"If I know you, Farrel," said Donzey, "all that showing of the teeth means that you are about to be real unkind to someone. It wouldn't be me, would it?"

"In a way," said the sheriff. "I'm goin' to bust up your place a little. You won't mind that, will you?"

"Nah," said Donzey, wondering what this was all about. "What are you going to bust up, what with, and why?"

"Answerin' your questions in order," said Farrel, grinning hugely, "Whatever gets in my way while I'm playing, a certain Mr. William Kelley, and you know as well as I do."

"Oh," Donzey rubbed his hands together. "So he's coming here? Or are you having him shipped by express?"

"He's coming of his own free will. He dropped into my office this morning and breezed up the place with a lot of noise about my not finding out who his wife ran away with. She's dead and he don't care about that. What makes him mad is that all these years he's been supporting a woman who— You know Bill Kelley."

Donzey felt a little sick. "How can a man be so rock-bottom lousy?"

"Aw, he's been practicing for years. Anyhow, I calmed him down and told him I knew a feller . . . that's you . . . who had found out who was in the car with his wife. I told him to come over at eight-thirty and see you. You can shove along now or stay and see the fun. This is the one place in town where I know I can do what I want without being interrupted."

"Which is—"

"Just what happened to Eula. She was rushing along in her car; she turned over and got all smashed up. I'm goin' to turn him over and smash him up." Farrel's smile was positively childlike.

"I'll stick around and watch," said Donzey. "By the way—" He hesitated.

"What?"

"I do know who was in the car with Eula."

"Yeah? Who?"

Donzey told him. "You don't say," said Farrel. "Well, well. Skull an' a scythe, an' all that?"

"Nah," said Donzey. "That's just a picture somebody drew. Looks as much like Him as a political cartoon does of a presidential candidate." The doorbell rang. "Farrel," said Donzey quickly, "I want him to see Eula's bone picture. Of all people in the world, he ought to appreciate it the most. Please."

Farrel said thoughtfully. "That'll be O.K. Then I don't have to explain nothin'. When the machine's through, I'll start, and he'll know just why."

Donzey went to the door and let in a superbly tailored gray sports suit with a pin-checked topcoat which contained an overload of pig eyes, flabby jowls and a voice like a fingernail on a piece of slate. Bill Kelley stamped past Donzey as if he were a butler or even a photoelectric door opener. He had apparently started griping even before he rang the bell, because he entered in the middle of a sentence.

"—come to a hovel like this on a wild-goose chase just because a fool of a sheriff can't get any information. I'm going to find out how much of my taxes goes to keep that fellow in office, and get an exemption. I'm the public, dammit, and I ought to be able to deal with a public servant. Hello, Farrel. What's all this nonsense, now?"

Farrel's voice cut through Kelley's because it was so deep and so very quiet. "That little man behind you is the guy I was tellin' you about. He's seen the man in Eu . . . Mrs. Kelley's car."

"Oh. Well? Well? Speak up, man. Who was it? If he's in business, I'll break him. If he's on relief, I'll have him taken off. If he's the kind of worthless tramp Eula would probably take up with, I'll hire some muscles I know to take care of him. Well? Well?"

"You can see him for yourself, *Mr.* Kelley," said Donzey evenly.

"I don't want to see him!" stormed Kelley. "Is he here?" He peered around.

Donzey had a flash of him grunting and wallowing in mud. "Not exactly. Sit down over there, and I'll show you a sort of moving picture."

Kelley opened his mouth to protest but found himself lifted off the floor, swung around and dropped into a chair. He squealed indignantly, saw Farrel's great horse face hovering close to his, turned a pinkish shade of gray and shut his mouth.

"Easy, Farrel," said Donzey gently, and put the earphones on Bill Kelley. Rummaging through his new filing cabinet, he clipped a specimen onto the machine and turned on the switch. Kelley's eyes closed.

They stood looking at their prisoner.

"Farrel—" said Donzey smoothly. The sheriff looked up. "What I was saying before he came . . . I've been wondering if it isn't the sight of Death that actually takes the . . . the soul out of a man."

Farrel grunted and turned back to Kelley. He was following the man's mind through that tragic maze of Eula's life. His jaw muscles kept knotting and slackening, beating like a heart.

Kelley suddenly stiffened. His eyes opened wide— so wide that the lids seemed about to fold back on themselves. The man's horrified gaze was directed at them, but they both sensed that he saw neither of them. For a full minute no one in the room moved.

"He's seen the show," muttered Farrel. "What's he

doing—stalling?" Then he realized that Kelley's staring eyes weren't looking at anything any more.

Donzey nodded. "Yup," he said, "it's seeing Him does it."

"What's the matter with him?"

"Why," said Donzey, "I reckon he climbed into the car with Eula. You see, I didn't set the time switch."

"Oh," said Farrel. He went and lifted up Kelley's wrist. "*Tsk, tsk.* Whaddye know. This here guy's up an' died on us. Heh! In a automobile accident that happened more'n a week ago!"

LIKE YOUNG

Here in the moonlight I sit, assigned to write an ode.
I won't write an ode. I'll write . . . I'll write what
happened instead. I'll never write another ode. I'm
a throwback. I'm a grinning savage, as of this day.
And they won't believe me, and they'll laugh—or they
will believe me, and then by the powers I think I'll
laugh. I think I will. I think I can.

Or cry. I think I can.

I know: I'll write it with all the background, just
as if there was somebody left on earth who hadn't
lived with it up to this moment. I just want to see if
one narrative can contain all of an enormity like
this.

The Immune—that's what we're called. But that's a
misnomer. We got it, all of us. It's just that we didn't
die of it. So, although Mankind was dead, we weren't
just yet.

Mankind was dead . . . Humanity wasn't. I guess
these things are open to definition. There were, by
the time we got them all together, six hundred and
four of us left of all the billions. We were all strong
and healthy, and most of us young. We could live,
learn, love. We could not propagate. So much for
Mankind.

We were, all of us, devoted to a single idea, and that was that Humanity should not perish. Humanity in the sense of aspiration, generosity—if you like, nobility: that was what we were dedicated to preserve. It was too late for us to use it. We'd only just realized what it was, when the new encephalitis appeared Perhaps we realized it *because* the encephalitis appeared. However we came by it, we had it, and we had to pass it on, or it was all too ludicrous a tragedy.

We decided to give it to the otters.

Like many another simple truth, the fact that the otters would be the next ones had been obvious and undisclosed. We were bemused by the fact that other animals—dogs, for example, and the higher apes, and (remember how exciting that was?) the contemplative porpoise—they all had intelligences like ours, in kind if not in quality. It was possible to think like a porpoise, or like a dog. It was a high conceit indeed to assume that the Next One would have an intelligence like ours. Once we were ready to discard that cocky notion, it became clear that the otter, a tool-using animal far earlier in its evolution than we had been, and possessed of a much more durable sense of humor, was logically our successor.

We despaired for ourselves; I want to make that quite clear. Our mourning was deep and bitter. But it must be made quite as clear that we passed through this mourning and emerged on the other side, as befit our maturity. We emerged late, and, for ourselves, uselessly; but emerge we did, mature we had become. You see what we were, for all our individual youth. We were the Elders of earth, and carried our insigne with a very real dignity. Too, we were each of us, all of us, wealthy and powerful beyond the wildest imag-

inings of anyone, ever—there were so few of us, so well
trained, with such resources (and no need to save).
Any of us could wave a hand and move a mountain.
Yet the big thing—the real thing—was that sense of
purpose and of dignity we had brought through the
terror and the death; a greater purpose, and a dignity
more real, than (but for a feeble flicker or two)
mankind had ever known before. Proud we were, of
course; but pride is a silly little word to use for such
a thing. Humbly, we liked ourselves. And it was this
above all we were dedicated to keeping alive. The
otters would have civilization, with or without us,
probably, but the achievement of this ultimate *dignity*
—ah, that was something we alone could teach them.
Only a Man could reach that height. Death gave us
this noble knowledge. Life—the New One's life—gave
us this purpose. And now they would have it in their
own lifetime.

And what a task it had been! For we were too
advanced, and the otters far too primitive, for us to
impress anything upon them while we shared the
earth with them. We would be dust for many
thousands of years before they began to communicate
even with one another. We had no intention of speed-
ing up their pre-history. Let them be what they were,
strong, adaptable, ubiquitous. Let them content
themselves with floating on their backs, holding shell-
fish on their chests, cracking them open with a stone,
until the day came when of their own accord they
found that was not enough. Let them kindle their
own light.

But we were determined that once it was burning
it should never flicker or dim. There would be no
dark ages for the otters. We would reduce basic
knowledge to its essence, put these in the most un-

derstandable form, and leave them like milestones (a statement and a promise, each) along the way.

For the milestones we chose the new alloy 2-chrome-vanadium-prime, which came to be called bicrovalloy. (Ah, what cities that might have built!) Properly fabricated, it could be formed into rods, bars, sheets; once irradiated, it would not, almost could not, change its form or state. This was no molecular lattice, nor even a net of atoms. It can best be described as a matrix of nuclei. Then thirty-foot sheets, supported only at the edges, could bear thousands of pounds at the center without bending more than a few thousandths. A hundred feet of quarter-inch rod, held horizontally by one end, showed no detectable sag. Drawn to a point, it would write on diamond as on wax; plates of it cooled to within a few thousandths of a degree of absolute zero and—or—raised to twenty million degrees, showed only a slight improvement of their finish. And what a finish! Silver-gilt, with a touch of peach . . .

On plates of bicrovalloy, then, man's wisdom was scribed. The task was enormous, but it was the only task we had. We had first to amass the necessary knowledge, then to distill it (and distill it again, and again, and again), and finally to codify it in such a way that the new race, the parameters of whose intelligence we could know only vaguely, would when ready for it be able to take and use it. When they had mastered fire, they must have ceramics. When they began working metal, they must have alloying and heat treatment. At a certain point in this mastery, they must be given knowledge of the power of steam. And so on. But nothing, if possible, before they were ready.

Placement of bicrovalloy plates, bearing the pertinent simple illustrations, in pottery-clay pits was self-evident, concealing them in likely lodes of minable metals was not so easy, for they must be hidden far enough down to make sure that their discovery was no accident. We gave language, numbers. And the ultimate secrets—ethical, spiritual as well as technological—these must be triply concealed, so that they would come out as a series of revelations; each a discovery, each a hint of the next, with everything in our power done to ensure they get it neither too soon nor, through over-concealment, not at all.

And so it was that the four equations of Einstein's General Field Theory, together with Heisenberg's addenda, were placed in the most inaccessible vault of all—in the mantle of the earth itself, in the bottom of the great bore under two miles of ocean where, in the twentieth century, we had reached our peak as engineers, seekers after knowledge. I need not go into the details of this ultimate achievement. For all our dedication, our immense resources, and our newer techniques, it was far harder for us to reach the bore than it had been for our forefathers to dig it.

The concealment of this final bicrovalloy plate was (it seemed at the time) our climatic conquest. I look back on those days with affection and sadness. It was a time of contemplative pride. We kept busy, of course, but our work was done. We had, in a fashion, survived our own death. We existed in a timeless moment, neither afterlife nor immortality, after the end of one great flowering and before the beginning of another. Humankind, the very death of humankind—that was behind us. The otters had not even begun; this was eons before their birth as the Next Ones.

So in this period we walked proudly, humbly conscious of our true usefulness and nobility. We had carried the torch.

And then—

Then De Wald produced the last equation.

De Wald had worked ceaselessly even before our project had begun, even before the first recorded case of the new encephalitis had claimed the first of its billions of victims. His material was the remarkable mathematical achievements of Heisenberg, and his goal a single expression which would not only encompass Einstein's four, but which would distill even Heisenberg's into something as clear as $e=mc^2$.

We had conferences and excited discussions, of course, but they were ritual (we had time for ritual then, and a great liking for it); everyone knew what was to be done. We had known because of the supreme *rightness* of such a discovery at such a time. Some talked about poetic justice and some about God; myself—I am not a scientist—I attributed it to Art. For our kind to end with a whimper, to be proven futile, or to have our work left in any way unfinished—this was Bad Art. De Wald's discovery, on the other hand, coming at just this time, was Art at its peak. One might almost say it justified everything, viewed objectively—even the tragic death of mankind. In a million years, through the eyes of another species, this would be the greatest story ever told . . .

Joyfully we set about the sizable task of recovering the now outdated set of bicrovalloy plates from the very flesh of the earth's body. And meanwhile the new plate was prepared—the old one could not be changed or added to, of course. Oh, it was good, good to be back at work again!

Then we were ready for the final placement. This of all times was the time to have a ceremony, and we planned a beautiful one. Grogerio himself would compose special music, and naturally no one but Fluger would design the dais on which the recovered plate and the ultimate one would lie side by side during the ceremony. And I was not in the least surprised when they came to me for an ode. Not in the least reluctant, either: for if created art comes from inspiration, surely there was enough and to spare in such an assignment.

I requested that I be left alone at the beautiful seaside spot on the night before the ceremony. I had already done a draft of the ode, but I knew what that vigil would do for the final version.

And indeed, the whole mood of the place and the time was perfect for such an effort. The last of the people left late in the afternoon, and I made myself comfortable in a spot where I could, at a glance, take in sea and sky, the silver beach and Fluger's beautiful dais, raised on two of his dizzying, gravity-defying arches. The *rightness* I mentioned earlier—this was a case in point. It has been said many times that neither a Fluger arch nor bicrovalloy could exist without the other.

And the sun went down in a blaze: how right! Even as we . . .

And in the east, a leaching of the firmament, and the loom of the moon . . . to be a new light on earth . . .

Then, wonder of wonders, there was a splash in the whispering surf and a small blackness oozing through the illumined dark. Oh, I thought, awe-struck: it can't be, but . . . yes; nothing could be more right . . . and then the moon struck upward with its metal edge, and cracked the cup of darkness, and I could see I was right in this rightness—it was a large male sea-otter snaking through the sand, working up toward the dais.

Exactly facing me, and not thirty yards away, he froze; had I not known where he was, I might have taken him for a hummock of sand or its deepening shadow. But I did know where he was, and in the growing light I could see the sensitive twitch of his comic mustache. I was not deceived as to the subject of his gaze, either, for I know his kind. An otter never looks directly at anything, any more than a bird does. One eye was regarding his beloved sea, and the other the dais. I, directly ahead of him, was unsuspected. And how perfect a picture this made, in all its symbolisms . . . how very right!

He turned in his quick lithe way and scuttled toward the dais, occasionally stopping in the otter's brief sudden pauses, as if one of his motivating wires were loose at the battery.

Silently, bemused and bemagicked, I followed. For in a moment like this, it must be so; it must be so: I alone—I, possibly the most perfectly qualified person on Earth and in all history to appreciate such a priceless picture, I would see this minion of the far-distant New Ones in the very shrine of all that was highest of Humanity.

And of course I was right—I was right—what could go wrong with such an enchantment? All the Powers of all the Souls of all Good Art would not permit anything, in such a moment, but what was right.

The otter, when at last I had crept round the dais and up behind the curtains and could see him, crouched motionless before and between the two bicrovalloy plates, the one just recovered, bearing Einstein's and Heisenberg's revelations, and the other which had just been fabricated to replace it.

I thought (a very whisper of a thought, lest I think too loudly and ripple this tableau): Are you praying, little one?

The otter rose suddenly on his hind legs and put his forepaws on the reclaimed plate. He seemed, in his clumsy, fumbling little way, to be caressing its surface. And the strangest feeling came over me, of shame, of that special kind of guilt one feels on having committed a faux pas, a *gaffe,* an in-itself petty kind of social offence which nonetheless it is acutely painful to remember. I felt like an intruder, a spy of the most ignorant and clumsy sort. To spare myself any more to brood on in the future, I removed the one wrong thing in that symphony of rightness—myself. Noiselessly I sank down behind the curtain and slipped into the sand below, and I was congratulating myself on being perhaps alone among men to have such perfect sensibility.

Rather than disturb him at whatever accidental orisons he was performing up there above me, I sat quietly until at last I saw him scampering off toward the sea. He had snatched up some bit of trash or jetsam from somewhere, and I saw him digging at the water's edge with it. I could just make out the two plump clams he unearthed, and then he was gone into the surf. I rose to catch, perhaps just once more, a single last glimpse of this creature, fellow to my most magic moment, and (as was only right) I did. He was floating joyfully on his back in the moonlight, with a clam on his strong chest. He struck it deftly with his crude tool, gulped it from the shattered shell, threw his unwanted trash upward into the moonlight, and was gone beneath the waves.

I gazed after the graceful clever little rascal, loving him . . . and turned toward my vigil-spot, all abrim with inspiration . . . and had I gone there, I surely should have written one hell, one hell of a *hell*uva ode . . . but instead I strode back up on the dais, to relive that incredible moment.

In the brilliant moonlight I gazed down at the shrine of humanity, all its dignity and its worth, and at all the meanings of this mighty gesture of faith in the life that had been and the life that was to be, when my eyes took in . . . took in what, some unmeasured time later—it might have been an hour— my mind was able to take in . . .

. . . just to the right of Einstein's brief immortal perfect statement of mass-energy conversion, the comment:

WELL, SOMETIMES

written on, *written into the bicrovalloy plate.*

And there were two corrections in the Heisenberg statement, strikeouts and carelessly scribbled figures which seemed to have been scribed deep in the impervious metal by a single small foreclaw . . .

But it was what had been done to the new De Wald plate that dealt me that blinding blow, from which I recovered (was it an hour later?) so slowly. For under that climactic, breathtaking achievement of intuitive mathematics, that most transcendental of all human statements, the De Wald Synthesis, the otter had scrawled:

NONSENSE!

I write no more odes. As for you who find this, and the plates which are its proof, do as you will. Have a suicide wave if you like. Or gather round in chittering groups and make wild surmise about the true source of the encephalitis which destroyed us, and great agonized guesses as to whether the otter was truly not quite aware of my presence and the significance of these plates and this whole occasion, and as to whether he and his kind are or are not impatient for our little remnant, with all our powers and resources, to be broken and maddened and die and go away. Or send your divers out if you like, to salvage that which he used to crack a clam—it's out there, not far—and prove to yourself that it is indeed the corner he broke off the De Wald plate with his bare paws; pick it up and fit it back again and pass it around and turn your silly laboratories loose on it. Maybe some of you will finally begin to roar with laughter, sob with merriment, as I have done to the point of exhaustion and helplessness, unable to get out of your minds the enormity of this one ridiculous fact: How *childish* is his handwriting! . . . so go do any of these things, or none of them, or something, out of the vast store of your pride and knowledge, of your own devising.

But me, I'm a joyful throwback . . . I'm one with my eager ancestors:—I'm going hunting.

DREAM SNAKE

Vonda N. McIntyre

"Rich in character, background and incident—
unusually absorbing and moving."
Publishers Weekly

"This is an exciting future-dream with real
characters, a believable mythos and, what's
more important, an excellent readable story."
Frank Herbert

The *"haunting, rich and tender novel"** of a
unique healer and her strange ordeal.
* Robert Silverberg

A Dell Book $2.25   (11729-1)

Dell Bestsellers